To Catch A Spy

To Catch A Spy

Anne Kimbell

Writers Club Press
San Jose New York Lincoln Shanghai

To Catch A Spy
All Rights Reserved © 2000 by Anne Kimbell

No part of this book may be reproduced
or transmitted in any form or by any
means, graphic, electronic, or mechanical,
including photocopying, recording,
taping, or by any information storage retrieval system,
without the permission in writing from the publisher.

Writers Club Press
an imprint of iUniverse.com, Inc.

For information address:
iUniverse.com, Inc.
620 North 48th Street, Suite 201
Lincoln, NE 68504-3467
www.iuniverse.com

The political events and characters in this book are purely
fictional and bear no relationship to anyone living or dead

ISBN: 0-595-12927-7

Printed in the United States of America

*To my careful readers and reviewers
Chris, James, Sally and Tom*

Chapter One

They say spring is the best time of the year in Paris to recruit a spy. The girls on the Champs Elysee have taken off their heavy winter coats and are in their budding phase. It's a good time to dangle a dangerous job in front of a reluctant recruit. The sap is rising.

Sam smiled ruefully, and rubbed his cheek, rough with a stubble of beard after another long day in the Defense Attaché's office at the American Embassy. No time to shave before he met his contact. Though "contact" was not exactly the right word for Rick. It might have been in Prague ten years ago. But now Sam was playing a long shot…and he knew it.

He looked down at the card in his hand. It was on heavy card stock, and slightly larger than usual. Trust Rick to get things right. From his perfectly cut tweed jacket, to his own special brand of aftershave to his cool good looks and athletic charm. He looked and behaved so correctly that no one ever found out exactly what it was he did. Sam was counting on the fact that the charm still worked, and that his operative's instincts were still intact after ten lazy years selling chemicals to private industry.

The bistro at the corner of Rue de la Verite was almost deserted at this hour of the afternoon, except for an old man sipping his Pernod and watching the parade of spring dresses outside the window through watery eyes. Sam lowered his girth into a seat in a darkened corner, depriving himself of a view of the girls, and focusing his highly developed talent of persuasion on the job at hand.

He had found a hook to catch Rick but he had to use it quickly. The assignment was too delicate and too dangerous to send an amateur. Yet, when Rick had left the service ten years ago, he had made it clear that he didn't want to play anymore. More than that, he had insulted enough of the top brass to make sure that no one would ask him again. He was a black sheep, a cast out and just right for the job.

Sam leaned back, ordered a glass of the Pernod and waited. Patience had always been one of his virtues. Now that he was ready for retirement, he could feel it ebbing. Rick had to take this assignment. There was no one else immediately available and too much was at risk to wait.

*   *   *

Rick Harrison walked briskly along the tree shaded Boulevard Monmartre. His eyes narrowed against the dying sunlight of a spring afternoon. He cursed himself silently for agreeing to meet Sam Shepherd. It was a stupid thing to do, and Rick prided himself on never making stupid moves. In fact, he rarely made any moves these days that weren't calculated to increase either his net worth, or his ability to do just exactly what he pleased for the rest of his life.

Sam had come swimming out of his past, surfacing almost as if from a dream, with a simple request to meet him for a drink in a spot they had frequented another lifetime ago. Knowing Sam, there must be an ulterior motive, and unless the answer was spelled in megabucks, Rick just wasn't interested.

He slowed his pace as he reached the corner of Rue de la Verite. An old habit of self preservation made him check the people near the entrance; a mother with her two small children out for an afternoon stroll; a young couple arm in arm; and a teenager trying to light a cigarette. Rick smiled bitterly. These days it could easily be the teenager. He watched the boy for a minute, as he hunched his shoulders under his thin blue sweater and slouched around the corner.

Rick hesitated for a moment, then entered the bar and ordered a *vin ordinare* from the bored bartender. He caught his first glimpse of Sam out of the corner of his eye, portlier than he remembered, but still with the look of an aging cherub that fooled many people into not taking him seriously. A decided plus for someone in the intelligence community.

They glanced at each other, like two fighters squaring off for a rematch after ten years. Then Rick picked up his glass, and walked to the shadowy corner table where Sam sat and waited, wearing a puckish grin. To Rick's acute discomfort, Sam stood up and embraced him like a long lost brother.

"It's been a long time", Sam said. "Have you missed all the excitement?"

Rick looked around warily. He had always been a little afraid of Sam's jovial glee, and his being involved in clandestine work for the intelligence community. And he suspected that more than one job had short circuited because of Sam's delight in letting people know what position he occupied at the embassy. But he was also quick to do a favor for a friend. And after all these years, Rick needed a favor, an added reason for agreeing to this meeting.

After a few minutes of polite banter in French, just enough to give the impression of two old friends meeting for a *petit verre* before going home to their wives and families, Rick dropped his voice and spoke quietly in English.

"So what's the deal Sam? You didn't invite me here just to see the color of my eyes again."

Sam smiled, wryly." I hear you sell agricultural chemicals now for one of the big pharmaceutical companies, and that your territory is North Africa, the *Magreb*. That could be of interest to us."

"You in the market for fertilizer?" Rick responded, narrowing his eyes and lighting a cigarette.

"No, but some friends of mine in Tunisia could use a little help. A week or so of your time, collect some information, perhaps a document or two, and leave somewhat richer for your trouble."

Rick leaned back in the booth, and for the first time he almost smiled.

"You're offering me a week in Tunis, all expenses paid. What if the PLO, or one of the right wing Muslim organizations hear about this?"

Sam stopped smiling. "They won't hear about it, if you're careful. And if you're smart, you can be in and out before anyone knows you're there. You can even sell a few chemicals, or fertilizer, or whatever you're selling, on the side."

"Any reason that you can think of that I should do this for you?"

"Don't do it for me, or for your country, or for money, do it for yourself."

"*Merde*, Sam. That man died and went to hell a long time ago. But thanks for the vote of confidence in a middle aged chemical salesman."

"Rick, a middle aged chemical salesman is just what we need in Tunisia right now, with some very special Eastern European scientists meeting in Tunis, for what we know not for sure, but we need to know, because these same chemicals innocently used for fertilizer can be used for more lethal purposes, and the scientists involved in this meeting in Tunisia are not fertilizer specialists!"

Rick finished his wine with a grimace of distaste, rose to his feet and extended his hand. "Sam, no more of those games for me, so count me out on this one".

Sam clasped the extended hand, while holding out a white card, embossed with the seal of the United States of America, with the other.

"Call me if you change your mind. And best regards to Melanie and to Robbie".

Rick took the card. It was hard to keep his hand from shaking. The bastard knew, and that was why he had tracked him down, and invited him here in the first place. He knew that Robbie had disappeared somewhere between Morocco and Tunisia. And he was offering his help. But as always…it was conditional. Remembering Melanie's voice on the phone this morning, he was tempted. But not enough to let Sam know that he had won…not right away anyhow. Let him sweat it out for a day or so. "I'll call you", he said, dropping a hundred franc note on the table. "The drinks are on me".

Rick caught a cab and went directly back to his hotel in a discrete neighborhood, within walking distance of the Champs Elysee. His phone was ringing as he entered the room. The antique sound of Paris telephones annoyed him. In fact, almost everything annoyed him since Melanie's call this morning. Why had she let the kid go off on his own this summer? Seventeen was no age to go tramping around Africa, and the *Magreb* in particular, with a bunch of kids, whose only experience of life came from a high priced prep school. Algeria and Libya certainly wouldn't be safe, even though Morocco and Tunisia might be.

He picked up the phone on its final ring, just in time to hear the operator telling his ex-wife that he wasn't there. He had a moment's instinct to skip the whole mess. Melanie had raised Robbie with her father's money, and her father's help. After all, Robbie's grandfather was Duke Weston, New York's super industrialist, and had business interests all over the world, including North Africa. Let them get him out of trouble.

Despite himself, her voice on the other end of the line sounded good. Perhaps it was just his male satisfaction in having her ask him for help. Besides, she was paying for the call, and being emotional on the long distance telephone had always been one of her strong points. Particularly when she needed something. But this time the tears sounded real.

Rick loosened his tie and sat gingerly on the usual fragile, small, pink, satin chair, while he listened. Their son Robbie had disappeared in Tunis two weeks ago, saying he was going to visit some friends in Sidi Bou Said. There had been no trace of him since, no ransom note and the Embassy had been unable to help. Could Rick please go and make some inquiries through his friends in government in Tunisia?

"I just know that he's in some kind of terrible trouble. It's our fault for not staying together, and raising him in a family".

On this familiar guilt ridden note, Rick quickly made his excuses and hung up the phone. Melanie was going to get her way again. He was going to Tunisia.

*   *   *

Robbie Benson Harrison, The Third, woke from a drugged sleep to find himself in an unfamiliar room, lit only by a window high up in the wall, covered with an intricate iron grill work. His head ached, and he had trouble focusing his eyes. He seemed to be wearing some kind of long, dirty dress and his feet were bare. He struggled to get up, only to find that one ankle was tied to the bed. A voice shouted at him harshly, in Arabic, and, when he continued to struggle to free himself, he heard a noise and everything went black.

His captor smiled, showing only three teeth, and then as the call to prayers began, silently prostrated himself toward Mecca.

Chapter Two

Sam Shepherd stayed a few minutes in the bistro after Harrison left. He had come to the age when he enjoyed savoring the last sip of his aperitif. And it was pleasant to observe the girls in their summer dresses. He contemplated having another glass, and then decided against it. Once he had finished this last assignment with Rick as his runner, he was going to retire, pay off that property in Arkansas and fish and hunt to his heart's content. He took out a card, and addressed an envelope to Rick at the hotel where he had located him, enclosing an open ended airline ticket to Tunisia, and a large amount of cash. As he left the bistro, he handed the envelope to a nondescript man in a green *deux chevaux*, with instructions to drop it off at Harrison's private little hotel just off Avenue Wagram.

When Harrison came down from his room for dinner, the lobby was crowded with a group of American tourists, who had just arrived, and who hadn't yet been assigned their rooms. The room clerk tried to get his attention over their heads, in what she evidently felt was a breach of etiquette for a French woman. When she failed, she was reduced to raising her voice, as he descended the worn carpeting.

"Monsieur Arrison has a packge.", she intoned over the heads of the tourists, who were getting more vocal about being ignored.

Harrison took the fat envelope from her, and shoved it into his breast pocket. Time enough to examine it away from the curious glances of his fellow countrymen, and the receptionist's encouraging smile. He was used to the attention of women, and at this place and time, he no longer found it flattering. He was still angry with himself for letting Melanie's call get to him. But he knew that if his son was in trouble, as a father, he had to make an effort to help him. Since the company was expecting him to make a trip to the *Magreb* in the next few weeks anyway, beginning the journey earlier in Tunisia wouldn't seem out of line. But staying there for more than a few days in each country was going to take some explaining. He glanced at his watch. It was much too late to call the states; a fax to the head office would let them know of his plans by morning. He'd have to see how soon he could get a flight.

It was raining lightly outside, and the streets were shiny under the yellow street lights. Harrison turned up his collar, and walked briskly towards the Champs Elysee, hoping to find a cafe open, where he could get a simple steak and fries, and avoid a full course evening meal. The air was crisp, and he gave himself the luxury of enjoying being in Paris. He had visited and stayed in the city many times in his career, and it never ceased to tantalize him.

Even here in the center of the tourist district, there was a feeling of excitement that even years of familiarity couldn't dissipate. A young couple walked past him, arms around each other, their black leather jackets and hair styles making them practically indistinguishable. Rick had a moment of *deja vu*. What would it be like to be that young again and that expectant? He couldn't imagine. Since his marriage to Melanie had gone bad, he had lived like a monk, paying for sex occasionally in preference to getting entangled. But Paris was the one city where it felt strange to be alone.

He ducked into a cafe which advertised a plat du jour of steak, *pommes frites* and salad for a decent price, and after he ordered the special with a glass of wine, took the fat envelope out of his pocket. It was easy to spot Sam's scrawl on the outside. He saw the amount of money, and the plane ticket. A telephone number was written on the ticket envelope. It wasn't much of a surprise that the ticket was to Tunis, and that Sam had baited the trap with a sizable amount of cash. But what exactly was it that the old fox wanted him to do? Posing as an irate American father demanding that the Embassy persevere in finding his son? That would be easy enough to do. It was whatever that followed that would be dicey, and once he pocketed the money, he was hooked again into a career that he thought he had abandoned once and for all.

Should he risk another meeting with Sam? His instinct told him that he was safer staying as far as possible from a known U.S. intelligence officer. Whoever he was going to have to deal with in the Magreb was bound to be well informed. He risked less, if he could get in and out fast, and get the job done. But he wanted more information from Sam. The days were over when he enjoyed risking his life just for the hell of it or to fulfill some sort of macho dream from a lonely boyhood spent reading adventure comic books by a flashlight under the bedcovers.

Serve the old devil right if I took the money and ran, Harrison mused. Wonder how many of his operators have had the guts to do that? He'd probably sick the IRS on me. He smiled wryly, stuffing the envelope back in his pocket, without counting it. He considered walking back to the hotel through the silent streets, but took a taxi instead. He roused the drowsing night clerk, and asked for a safety deposit box. Then after locking the envelope in it, he spent a restless night dreaming of being chased through the streets of Paris by two men on black motorcycles. In his dream, he turned and shot at one only to discover that the man lying under a streetlight in a pool of blood was his son, Robbie.

*   *   *

Sam walked south on Rue de la Verite, heading towards the Embassy. For a widower who had given most of his life's energy to his work, there wasn't much else to do in the evening but go back and check the cables. It was morning in Washington and Sam always liked to see what was going on, so that he could have the evening to think it over and mentally draft a reply. He had discovered early in his career, that his ability to write long detailed, and somewhat obscure intelligence reports, was a talent which kept his supervisors in Washington off his back most of the time. He kept them at bay with words when he didn't need their advice and was able to get them on his side as easily, when he needed help or more funds to operate with. The situation developing in Tunisia was one of the times he wanted to keep them guessing, until he was sure that he had all the facts.

Like most good intelligence officers, Sam pieced together much of what he knew, by information which was available to most intelligent people, if they knew how to read and were canny listeners. It also helped to have a few paid informers, and to discount about sixty percent of what they told you. But, every now and then, you got a scrap of truth, which, pieced together with other scraps gave you an outline. The one he had put together in the last few weeks about the possibility of production of weapons of mass destruction, including chemical and biological warfare products, in North Africa was chilling.

He received the salute of the Marine guard on duty at the front gate of the Embassy, smiling at the boy's immaculately pressed uniform and fresh farm look. He would certainly have something to tell his grandchildren about life in Paris some day—if he lived to tell about it.

Sam paused outside his office, checking the lock automatically to see that it hadn't been tampered with. The door to the Ambassador's office was ajar, and there was a faint light coming from under the door. Unusual that the old man was working this late, but the office at night was often a welcome respite from the endless cocktail and dinner parties. Things had been tense lately in the world situation, and Paris was feeling the shock waves.

If Sam's hunch was right, some country or splinter faction was about to emulate the weapon building of Iraq, but this time in a place closer to Europe. And all the signals were coming from the *Magreb*—it could be

Libya, but Morocco, Algeria or Tunisia were also likely candidates. Shipments of various chemicals, including possible fissionable materials, were going into North Africa. Libya and Algeria had ordered chemicals to make pesticides and insecticides, without having the factories to produce them locally, and these same chemicals, apparently, were capable of being turned into nerve gases. Egypt was ordering certain sophisticated triggering devices from Germany, ostensibly for missiles to launch their own communication satellites, but the devices were multi-purpose and could be used for more sinister purposes.

And now this report from Tunisia, that a right wing Muslim party was claiming the responsibility for an attack on their President's life. Reports were coming in from each of these countries that the groups responsible for the development of arsenals were the right wing elements, and that they were growing and becoming increasingly more militant.

But somewhere there had to be a leader. The shipments of material were too well planned, and too well coordinated, for them to be random. All signs pointed to Tunis, and to the coming together of diverse elements from several countries sometime in the next few weeks. Sam opened his file and took another look at the microfiche documents that he had been laboriously collecting. All signs pointed to one man. But he was so well known and so powerful that pulling the plug on him would be tantamount to cutting his own throat, unless he was absolutely sure. Nailing him was going to be Rick's job but the less he knew about it, the safer he was, for the moment.

He added Rick's card to the file, placing it in a folder marked, "pending" and carefully double locked the file drawer. He gave a cursory glance to the teletype machine pounding out the world's headlines, and to the fax to see if there were any late cables. He picked up two phone messages, and glanced at his watch. One was from Rick's ex-wife, Melanie. He smiled to himself. It was a bit late to return her call. That would have to wait until later.

Strange how all the elements had cooperated to give him Rick just when he needed him. Too bad about Robbie, but he was probably off somewhere with a girl, and just didn't want his mommie to know. He heard the fax beep twice, then begin to slip out its silent message. A certain high level German scientist was on his way to Tunis for an international symposium. Sam read the message and realized that the game had begun. With any luck Rick would get there first.

At six o'clock the next evening, the plane from Orly came in low over the Tunis airport. Rick stretched his cramped legs, and followed the pilot's instructions to *"attachez vos centures de securite."* As the plane banked, he could see the Tunis Hilton outlined against the setting sun, and rivaling the Cathedral of Saint Louis for first place on the skyline. The Cathedral was now a museum, a symbol of the Tunisians proverbial tolerance for all religions.

Rick was still angry with himself for taking on this assignment, but it fit in with his search for Robbie, all expenses paid. Sam's voice over the phone had been almost gleeful, but he hadn't given out much more information. Only that reservations had been made for him at the Tunis Hilton and that his contact would call him there, using the code name Sweetiepie. If there were any problems, or the contact didn't show, he was to call the number on the ticket envelope. A recording machine would answer, with a message which was changed daily. He was to ask for backup help, and it would be given, that was all.

Rick had memorized the number, then carefully chewed it into chewing gum consistency and put it into the ash tray at his seat. He had considered burning it, but since this was a non-smoking flight, he didn't want to risk setting off the smoke alarm in the toilet. He shifted in his seat, ignoring the comforting smiles of the motherly flight attendant, as she took his glass from him. "We're almost there, sir; please adjust your seat back." Rick smiled grimly. Even the flight attendants were getting older. What in the hell was he doing playing cops and robbers at his age? Ten years out of the business had made him soft. All he wanted now was a hot shower, and a line on Robbie. Then he was going to hand this assignment back to Sam on a platter.

The heat of the late afternoon enveloped him like a warm blanket, as he left the plane. The crowds, dressed in a combination of western and Arab garb, surrounded him, shoving, yelling and pushing, as luggage came down the chute. He found his bag, and wrestled it away from a determined porter, looking around for the taxi rank. A voice behind him said, in heavily accented English. "I carry bags, and get you to the hotel in my car. All one price. I very good driver."

Harrison waved the man away, almost without looking at him. It was his experience that taxi drivers, who met you at the luggage drop, were either more expensive or sent by someone else. He wanted to avoid either eventuality. The man was persistent, standing so close that Rick could smell his peculiar odor of sweat and spice. He was of medium height, and wore black trousers and a tattered, but clean shirt and a short embroidered vest. His eyes were black as olives and slightly crossed. He smiled at Rick engagingly, tugging at his valise. "I take you to the hotel cheap, sweetiepie", he said, finally wresting the suitcase from Rick's hand. "My name is Ahmed. I will be at your service."

The whole operation was a bit too amateurish for Rick's taste. But he decided to go along with it, to see if the man had any information to give him. In the beginning the ride toward the hotel, past the lake of Tunis, was uneventful. Ahmed drove with the radio at full blast, playing a wailing lament of Oum Kaltoum, and occasionally joining in a high falsetto. He honked at almost every other car on the road. Hardly an inconspicuous entry into the country, thought Harrison mentally squirming in his seat. Perhaps the man had used the code name by mistake. His English seemed rudimentary otherwise.

Instead of going directly to the hotel the taxi veered off in the direction of the Old City, driving through streets which became narrower and narrower as they neared its walls. When Harrison protested, Ahmed became grim faced and drove even faster. "I pick up something here for you," he said in explanation. He brought the car to a screeching halt outside a building that looked as though only its ornate nail studded door was holding it up. The street was deserted, except for two ancient men sitting on the sidewalk, drinking tea from a brass tea pot and tiny glasses.

"you wait here, sir", said Ahmed, as he opened the car door.

"Like hell, I will", answered Rick, grabbing the man's arm with one hand, and his suitcase with the other. "Take me to my hotel."

"I think someone meet you", said Ahmed, pulling back and looking toward the door. It opened slowly and a slender, blonde woman emerged, carrying a huge basket laden with parcels. She dropped the basket into the front seat of the taxi, and with a quick glance at Ahmed, grabbed Harrison's arm, and half pushed him back into the car. "Darling, how good of you to pick me up. I'm exhausted from shopping", she said glancing over his shoulder into the street beyond and giving him a kiss on both cheeks in the French fashion.

Harrison caught a whiff of jasmine perfume, as she pushed her way into the taxi beside him. She was rather attractive in a too-thin sort of way, and a closer look told him that she was not as young as he had first imagined. There were fine lines around her mouth and eyes, and a determined tilt to her chin. She looked Harrison over appraisingly, as the taxi veered wildly into the street while Ahmed drove in sync with an Arab love chant.

As they rounded a corner, she veered over against him, using the occasion to press a piece of paper into his hand. She spoke softly into his ear, while seeming to snuggle up against him. A sensation that, to his surprise, Harrison found not unpleasant. "I'm Janine, your contact at the Embassy. I'll try to fill you in at the Ambassador's reception tonight. In the meantime, Sam has arranged for me to get any information back to him through classified channels. Use this number to reach me. We can meet at the *Souk des Tinturiers*, number 10 if necessary. Ahmed knows the way."

Harrison glanced quizzically in Ahmed's direction. The woman nodded. "He knows only what is necessary, 'Sweetiepie', so use him cautiously." She straightened her rumpled linen skirt, and spoke in French to the driver. "You will drop me at my apartment now." She turned, and smiled beguilingly at Harrison. "I hope that you don't mind that your contact is a woman. It is a very safe cover in this country", she whispered in his ear.

The taxi stopped before an Arab style apartment building, set back from the street. In the dying light, Harrison could just barely make out the street name, and he memorized the look of the building. It was still heavily shuttered against the afternoon sun, and several grimy children played in the street in front of it. Janine barely waited for the taxi to stop, before she grabbed her heavy shopping basket from the front seat. "Thanks loads for the lift, darling. Mother says to check in with Dr. von Grantz at your hotel; he is supposed to arrive today." She blew him a kiss, and was gone into the silent building.

Well, at least now he had one name to put into the puzzle: von Grantz.

When she was gone, the taxi still held her tantalizing sent of jasmine perfume. Harrison leaned back against the seat, as the car sped through the thickening traffic. His head felt heavy, and he had a sense that all of this was rushing at him too rapidly. He must be out of practice. He needed a drink, a shower and a while to sort things out. Sam's methods were, to put it mildly, extraordinary. They reeked of a man who has thrown caution to the winds at the casino, and was betting his whole bankroll on rolling the hard eight one last time.

The trouble was that there just wasn't that much time. His only chance was to get whatever information Sam needed quickly, trade it for news of Robbie's whereabouts, and get out of Tunisia and back to his job before he got fired and Melanie lost out on a few months alimony. The thought of that gave him a sort of perverse pleasure, he was smiling as he walked into the foyer of the Hilton.

The foyer was large, vaulted and luminous, with a kind of ersatz elegance that Rick remembered from former visits. The smartly dressed hotel clerk greeted him effusively in French, and then shifted quickly to English, when Rick didn't respond. "We have been awaiting your arrival, sir. Just how long will you be with us?"

"*Ca depends*", Rick responded, just to keep the man on his toes. "Are there any messages?"

"Oh, yes sir", the clerk gushed, rolling his eyes. "I believe that it is from your Embassy."

Rick took the embossed envelope the man offered him, along with his room key and several cables from his head office. He pocketed the key, and with it the note Janine had given him in the taxi. He surveyed the lobby as he walked to the elevator. Nothing overtly unusual. Several Arab businessmen in correct navy blue suits and head cloths having tea in one corner. One gray haired man by the newsstand looking over the newspapers. No women at all. Not even women with children. Not in public places, not alone. It was a hell of a place to be a bachelor, Rick remembered. Perhaps that was what had made Melanie so appealing. But that was old news. Robbie was the problem now, as was Sam's scheme to score one last time before he retired.

He unlocked the door to his room and, after he had insisted on opening the shutters, giving the bellboy too large a tip. The room looked down on a brown, rolling hillside, and on the city of Tunis beyond. The last dusky pink light was settling over the city and in the distance, he could hear the shrill wailing of the call to prayers. The bellboy backed out of the room, smiling. Probably gone to find his prayer rug and a quiet place to prostrate himself towards Mecca five times. It must be a strange feeling to believe in anything that sincerely.

Rick loosened his tie, and glanced at the faxes from his company headquarters. Routine stuff, no question of why he had decided to spend a few days in Tunis "renewing old contacts". That was one of the perks of being a one man show in North Africa. As long as the orders rolled in, no one questioned too closely what he did with his time. He flipped open the large white envelope, and then poured himself a drink from the mini-bar in the corner of his room. It was from the Embassy. An invitation to a reception for a Dr. Helmut von Grantz, from the former East German Republic, and his colleagues from the United States Department of Agriculture. Rick glanced at his watch. The invitation was for this evening, and was the meeting place with Janine, to which she had alluded. He would have to arrive within the hour, but it would be worth it if he could get a line on von Grantz.

Freshly showered and shaved, he left his room at a quarter to the hour, giving himself just enough time to arrive after most of the other guests, and most certainly the guest of honor, who should be in the receiving line. The reception was at the Ambassador's residence in sidi Bou Said, on the outskirts of Tunis. When he got outside the hotel, Ahmed was nowhere to be seen. Somehow, Rick had been expecting him to be waiting. He hailed another taxi, and was treated to a ten minute ride, equally as wild as the one from the airport. Only the music was different, a French version of a current American hit, with only the beat recognizable.

The driver deposited him in front of a palatial villa, surrounded with gardens. The party was already in full swing. The sound of clinking glasses and polite conversation greeted him at the entrance, along with a young Foreign Service officer delegated to let in only those bearing invitations. Rick surrendered his and was ushered into the receiving line, where the Ambassador and his wife were holding court, along with three soberly dressed gentlemen, one of whom was Dr. Helmut von Grantz.

Von Grantz stood in the position of honor, next to the Ambassador, and shook Rick's hand with a military precision, that in an earlier time would have been accompanied by the clicking of his heels. He was of medium height, with a small beard, and wore tinted glasses, which half obscured his eyes, yet there was something about him that was troublingly familiar. He answered Rick's greeting in heavily accented

English, and his face showed nothing beyond polite boredom. Rick pulled himself away from the Ambassador's wife, who had a tendency to gush, and headed towards a group of men clustered around the bar.

He melted into the group, who were all wearing the standard, dark suited uniforms of men at official functions. On the whole, there were more men than women at the party, and the majority of women were European. Even here in liberalized Tunis, most of the Arab women stayed at home. The conversations around him were mostly in Arabic and French. He pretended to speak neither, and that way was able to eavesdrop most efficiently. What he discovered was that von Grantz and his colleagues ostensibly were here to make a study of agricultural uses of portions of the desert, and also to see what chemical materials might exist, or have to be imported, to be used in a project for manufacturing fertilizers, and pesticides in Tunisian factories.

It sounded as though part of the plan for the project was to use former East German chemists and researchers as participants in multi-national teams, helping developing third world countries maximize their resources. On the surface, it sounded like a fine idea. It occurred to Rick, as he listened, that it was a great chance for people with various shades of ideology not only to work together as a team, but to use the country they were doing research in as a cover for other activities.

Rick strolled away from the bar, just as the men he had been standing next to, began to regard him with a certain amount of curiosity. Pretending that he didn't understand their conversation worked for only so long. He saw a sullen looking young girl on the other side of the room in heated conversation with a man somewhat older than she. He drifted in her direction. She looked to be about Robbie's age. Despite her makeup and obvious attempts to look sophisticated she was still wearing her baby fat. The man was attempting to take her arm and she was resisting loudly.

As Rick got nearer, he could see that the girl was either drunk, or smoking something stronger than a regular cigarette. Catching Rick's eye, she plunged through the crowd toward him, pulling her body guard with her, like a small ship under full sail. The man resisted, but unwilling to make a scene, followed her like a large, obedient dog.

"You're new", she said, fixing Rick with the look of a spoiled child, who is used to getting what she wants. "What are you doing in this boring place, and how soon do you plan to leave?"

"Oh, I don't know, as soon as I get my business accomplished, I suppose." Rick responded lightly.

"And what is that?" she asked, slurring her words slightly, and fixing him with puppy dog brown eyes. Her guardian, or boyfriend, took her arm and tried to pull her away. Rick stopped him with a gesture.

"I'm here looking for my son, Robbie, who is about your age. He was traveling with some friends, and seems to have disappeared somewhere in the *Magreb*." Rick answered, candidly.

The girl looked startled, and for a moment almost sober. Then she looked up at the man beside her, who was watching her through half-closed eyes. She smiled foolishly, and lowered her eyes. "I'm always losing things, aren't I Brahim?," she giggled, and pulled the man with her over towards the bar.

Rick watched them walk away feeling frustrated. The girl had reacted at Robbie's name, but her protector wasn't going to let him get anything else out of her right now. He would have to proceed more cautiously, and make inquiries through official channels. But all that could take more time than was available. He had to get results, and he had to get them quickly, and it appeared that the girl, whoever she was, might possibly be able to help.

He turned to go, but the scent of jasmine perfume stopped him. Janine was standing behind him. He wondered how long she had been watching. "Playing with the Ambassador's daughter isn't allowed," she said, putting a well manicured hand on his arm, and leading him to a quiet corner of the garden. She was wearing a short, white dress and her ears were accentuated by large white-gold earrings that looked like lace.

Her face was scrubbed clean, except for a splash of bright pink lipstick. She looked thoroughly desirable.

Rick took the drink she offered him from a low table. "That was a quick change," he said, not bothering to cover the approval in his voice.

"I'm known for quick changes," Janine countered. "But watch yourself around the Ambassador's baby daughter, and her boyfriend. Word has it that she's bad medicine."

"Janine, in addition to doing a little job for Sam Shepherd, I am here looking for my son, and I think that she knows something about him."

Janine looked thoughtful. "If he's male, and attractive, and has been anywhere near Tunis, chances are you're right. But getting her to tell you anything will be a challenge. She ignores her father, hates her mother and her Arab boyfriend has got a leash on her at the moment." She looked over at him thoughtfully. "What do you think about von Grantz?"

"I recognize him from somewhere. The beard and glasses change him, but it's the same man. How long before he leaves town?"

"The team leaves for D'Jerba this week for a preliminary look at the various sites in the desert. Then they will make a full report later after they do a feasibility study of the area." She looked at him over the rim of her glass. "Want to go along?"

Rick narrowed his eyes. "Can Sam arrange that too?"

Janine touched his shoulder lightly, "No darling, but I can."

"Just like that?"

"Well it does help to work for the Commercial Attach, who is away on vacation. You can join their party as a business observer. Just a few days until you find out what von Grantz is up to."

"And what do I do when I find out? Send a camel with a message in its teeth."

"Oh, no," she said, earnestly, reacting as if the question had been serious. You relay it to our man in D'Jerba."

Rick looked her over carefully. "For starters, any idea what they might be up to?"

She gazed around the garden, then moved away from the shelter of high shrubbery to sit casually on the edge of a tinkling Arab fountain. Rick followed her. The sound of falling water would mask the rest of their conversation. Not that he expected bugs in the Ambassador's courtyard, but it didn't hurt to be extra careful.

"We don't know exactly, but von Grantz's arrival is matched by other scientists arriving in North Africa from other former Iron Curtain countries. We suspect that it is part of the Eastern European brain drain, but we aren't sure exactly what the purpose is, or who is masterminding it. On the surface, it all looks quite innocent. But someone has knowledge of these men's expertise, and their abilities place them in strategic positions. "She smiled up at him flirtatiously, as two men walked by, eyeing them curiously. Then she took his arm and, snuggling up to him, walked slowly toward the Residence.

And you think I'm going to solve this for you in just a few days?", Rick said, wryly, when they were inside the foyer.

"Your company is involved in all areas of the chemical business, and you know a lot about fertilizers, pesticides, insecticides, and pharmaceuticals, don't you? So you can at least go along, and ask the right questions."

"And while I'm waltzing around the desert, who is going to find my son?"

She looked at him soberly, dropping her polite cocktail party manner for a few seconds. "We have been making all the necessary inquiries, but the answer to that question seems to be somewhere in the desert, too. The boys were last seen near D'Jerba."

Rick grabbed her elbow, digging his fingers in, until she grimaced with pain. "Damn you", he hissed. "If you and Sam are risking my son's life to get me to play along, I swear I'll kill you both."

She leaned against him, her eyes suddenly cold. "If you do, you'll never find him. Because you can't do much in this country without our help. Think about it. I'll be in touch."

Chapter Three

Rick woke the next morning with the sun in his eyes, and a splitting headache. He had dined mostly on hors d'oeuvres at the Ambassador's party. After their brief conversation, Janine had ignored him for the rest of the evening, leaving him to find a cab and a solitary dinner. He hadn't been up to looking for any of his old haunts in Sidi Bou Said, the blue and white village above Tunis. He decided, over a strong cup of coffee, to go there again this morning, and see if any of the artists he once knew were still in residence. They might be able to provide a line on Robbie, particularly Ben Halim who had known him as a little boy. Robbie might have contacted him. It was a slim chance, but any chance, slim or not, was worth taking.

Fighting his way through cab drivers outside the hotel, he walked a few blocks and took the clattering, narrow gage trolley car which meandered its way to the foot of Bursa Hill, and then on to Sidi Bou. The trolley made frequent stops along the way, and Rick had time to admire the view of bougainvillea clad villas climbing up Bursa Hill, the site of ancient Carthage. To his right were the Roman baths, a symbol of the culture Rome had imposed on North Africa, a culture which survived here almost three hundred years after the fall of Imperial Rome.

It was hard to imagine anything sinister happening here on this beautiful morning. But Robbie's disappearance was real and von Grantz was real. And from past experience, he knew that Sam didn't send operatives off on wild goose chases. He was on to something big, something that had to do with the desert, and with whatever von Grantz and his team were looking for there.

The trolley jerked to a trembling halt. Rick jumped off one station early, just for the pleasure of stretching his legs and smelling the sun laden air. The Mediterranean stretched out on his left, deceptively placid at this hour of the morning. He began climbing the narrow, winding street that led to the center of the village. The tension in the calves of his legs felt good, and he accelerated his pace as he climbed.

Shop keepers were just beginning to open their shutters, and blue and white bird cages beckoned from vendor's stalls, along with a myriad of other merchandise. An old man, in a white cap and gown, greeted him gracefully in Arabic, gesturing towards his goods, "*Ahlan wa sahlan*", he said in welcome. Rick acknowledged the greeting, but kept walking. He didn't have the stomach this morning for graceful bargaining, and he didn't want to do it ungraciously. He owed that much to what he knew of Tunisian courtesy.

He quickened his step as he neared the top of the village. A small *taverna* was open selling cakes and tea, and hot, sweet Arab coffee in tiny cups. The proprietor was an elderly man with one eye, few teeth and what looked like a perpetual smile. Rick ordered a coffee, and sat down to catch his breath. Looking around, he realized that he no longer recognized the place. All of the buildings were whitewashed, all had blue shutters, and which one belonged to his friend he could no longer tell.

He sat for about half an hour, drinking his coffee and watching the town wake up. It was also a good excuse to make sure he hadn't been followed. The village had only one narrow street leading toward this square, and so far he was the only 'tourist' about. Two children led a sheep decorated with ribbons up the hill. It bleated and protested, making them laugh uncontrollably. Three elderly women covered their faces with their *safsaris*, as they walked by him, but otherwise, he might have been invisible.

It was a pleasant feeling. He could feel the muscles in his neck relaxing, for the first time in a week.

After a second coffee, he left a few coins on the table, nodded at the proprietor and rose to go. At the same time, a commotion erupted at the end of the street. A large rooster was loose, and had decided to take on the sheep in mortal combat. This provided enough diversion, so that Rick had time to stroll down the street, looking for the house number and name of his friend Ben Halim. His stroll took him down a narrow, winding alleyway, with an occasional breathtaking view of the bay of Tunis. The houses were so close together that they shared walls and roof gardens.

When he finally was sure that he had found the house, it was smaller than he remembered, and a bit further away from the center of the village. Ben's distinctive sign in Arabic and French, though, was still unmistakable. It hung outside a white washed two story villa, with jasmine framing the blue doorway. The door was bolted, but the shutters were just being opened by a young Arab girl. Rick decided to knock.

The girl anticipated his gesture and opened the door just as he raised his hand. She smiled shyly, and ushered him into a combination living room and studio, filled with the vibrant paintings that were Ben's signature. There was little furniture. One corner held a woven Tunisian rug in lavender and green, with colorful cushions piled on it, surrounding a small rose and green decorated table. She spoke to him softly in Arabic, gesturing toward the corner. When he looked blank, "Ben will come soon", she said in French. "Your name please?"

"Harrison", Rick said abruptly, the urgency of his mission overcoming his usual sense of courtesy. The girl looked stricken and hurried from the room. Rick realized then that she couldn't be more than twelve or thirteen. No reason for him to take out Robbie's disappearance on Ben's family. He walked around the studio, idly studying the paintings. Most of them were portraits of Arab men in stylized clothes. A few were of *safsari* clad women, and one or two were of the lovely young girl who had answered the door. He was studying one of these, when he heard a door open behind him.

He turned to face a heavy set Tunisian, wearing a long blue and white striped gelaba. "You have met my daughter, Lila", Ben said smiling. "She told me that a very rude man was here waiting to see me."

Rick smiled apologetically, and extended his hand. "Not a very civilized way to treat the daughter of a friend after so many years. But perhaps when you hear my story you will excuse me."

Ben smiled expansively." I shall, but she probably won't, for a while anyhow. Since her mother died, she takes herself very seriously as my hostess." He eased his broad girth down onto the cushions, and gestured for Rick to do the same. "Will you take coffee?"

The thought of a third cup of pure, sweet caffeine on top of no food was not appetizing, but Rick nodded acceptance. He knew better than to offend Ben Halim's household a second time. By the time that Lila had brought the coffee, Rick had told Ben of his divorce and of Robbie's disappearance somewhere in the Magreb.

"His round trip ticket was through Tunis, so I was hoping that you might have seen him. He was very fond of you and of Sidi Bou as a child. I thought he might have come here."

Ben looked troubled, handed Rick a cup of coffee, and then gestured for Lila to leave the room. She did so reluctantly. Rick made a mental note to send her a gift as soon as possible, to make up for this series of blows to her ego. When she was safely out of the room, Ben Halim leaned over and picked up a small sketch book lying on the floor. He flipped through it casually, and then handed it to Rick with a page opened. The face that looked back at him off the page was of a thin faced boy with a pony tail, and a scraggly excuse for a beard, but it was Robbie never the less. From the sketch, it looked as though he were wearing a gelaba.

"I saw him in Sidi Bou at a cafe with a group of friends and sketched him before I realized it was Robbie. I was taken by the expression on his face, and then shocked when I realized who it was. I tried to speak to him, but his friends were very inhospitable." He looked grave and took a sip of his coffee. "All I could get from them was that they were planning to go to Marrakech along the coast of Morocco, and then return to Tunisia later via the desert. That was over three weeks ago."

"That's about the last time his mother heard from him", Rick said playing with his coffee cup. "What did the people look like that he was with?"

Ben looked thoughtful. "Older than Robbie I would say," he paused thoughtfully. "Two of them spoke Arabic well. I would say they were either Algerian or Moroccan. One of the other boys had red hair and blue eyes, but he was also wearing a gelaba. "Here, I made a quick sketch of them." He tore a page out of his sketch book and handed it to Rick. It was a fluid line drawing of four young men, huddled around a cafe table. Two of them were clearly Arabic in countenance, and two were obviously Anglo Saxons, somewhat awkward in their gelabas. Ben had caught the humor of the American boys wearing Arab clothes, but he had also caught something sinister in the look of their two companions.

"Did you see them again?", Rick asked, feeling a tightening in the pit of his stomach.

"No", Ben replied, "but I heard from some friends in the village that they were staying here in Sidi Bou at the home of an Algerian whom no one knows much about. The house is just two streets below here. There is talk that he is selling *kief kief,* you know, 'Hash,' but so far the police haven't caught him at it. He seems to have a lot of visitors, most of them young male foreigners." Ben stopped and took a sip of his coffee. "I'm sorry to be the bearer of such troubling news my friend."

"It doesn't sound good", Rick acknowledged. After a little more talk, he rose to his feet and thanking Ben Halim for his time and for the coffee, he gave him his room number at the Hilton, should he pick up any more information either about Robbie or about his host. He also told him that he would be leaving in a few days for D'Jerba.

Ben shook his hand warmly, standing up with a slight groan, and a rustle of his gelaba. "Keep this sketch, if it will help, but be careful, my friend. There are many serpents in the desert these days. They strike suddenly. Trust no one in the South. And above all, I hope that you find your son. One's firstborn is precious".

Rick nodded, and walking toward the door, he folded Ben's sketch, and put it in his pocket. Lila glanced at him soberly, as she opened the door for him. Her gravity in saying goodbye, befitted a twenty year old. He thanked her graciously for the coffee, and, as he was leaving, was rewarded with just the hint of a smile.

Once outside the cool interior, he was greeted with blinding sunlight. Now the street was busy with people out for a morning stroll. The day was clear and fresh. On an impulse, he turned down the hill to the narrow street mentioned by Ben, to search out the house where Robbie had been staying with the Algerian. He didn't know what he expected to find, but he wanted something more concrete, before he talked to the people at the Embassy. Besides, he could move much faster in an unofficial capacity before he enlisted the Embassy's help. Perhaps more so before, than after.

A stroll down the narrow street revealed little that he hadn't known before. The house, where Robbie was supposed to have stayed, looked empty, with shutters still closed against the morning sunlight. He rang the bell, listening for footsteps inside, but none came. He walked to the end of the street, hoping to find a back entrance, but found a high wall surrounding the property in the rear, topped with pieces of jagged glass designed to stop marauders. He took careful note of the height of the wall. It would be difficult, but not impossible, to get over, and would require some tools and thick leather gloves. But that was a project best approached under cover of darkness.

For the moment it was better to play the role of a casual tourist enjoying the sights. He reminded himself to carry a camera the next time he came. It could be put to good use to document the heights of the wall, as well as giving him the tourist cover. For a moment, he thought that he caught sight of some movement in an upper window. Just then, a herd of goats, coming down the alleyway, persuaded him that it was time to leave. It was time that he called in at the Embassy, and made contact with the Commercial Attaché. He needed to cover his presence in Tunisia for the company's benefit, and see if he could do some business while he was here.

He called the Embassy from the hotel, and was told that Mr. Johnson was on home leave, but in the meantime, his duties were being handled by another officer. Could he come to the Embassy after two thirty, when he would be granted an appointment? Rick chafed at the delay, he wanted to get started looking for Robbie, and to do it as quickly as possible. Ben's news had made him very uneasy. Robbie with his good prep school ideals, would be fair game for someone who could sell him a political bill of goods, and a little hash at the same time.

* * *

Robbie opened his eyes, and looked around carefully. His mouth was dry, and his arms were numb from being tied together behind his back. He was in a room with only a crack of light coming in around the door. It smelled of camels. His red haired friend, Pete, was gone. There was a pile of clothes in the corner that looked like the ones he had been wearing when they were all picked up by the men in the truck, who had offered them a ride across the border into Algeria. Mohammed and Ali had talked with the men in Arabic and had been eager to take them up on their offer of transportation. Once in the truck their Arab friends' attitudes had begun to change. He remembered a fight and someone coming at him with a knife and then, nothing more. Wherever he was, he was alone. Robbie's head began to swim again and suddenly the light was gone.

* * *

Rick ate a quick lunch at the hotel coffee shop, and then realized that he still had an hour to wait before his appointment, because no one in Tunis finished lunch before two. He tried to read the paper, but found that his Arabic wasn't good enough or his patience long enough to translate more than the headlines. Much was being made of the visit of the former East German scientists to Tunis. Also, security was being tightened at all borders to keep out "subversive agents and drug traffickers."

There was the usual political hyperbole about the coming elections. However, he noticed that the ultra conservative Muslim party was still being excluded from the elective process. Pretty much business as usual. One item caught his eye. A chemical processing plant in D'Jerba was being enlarged to provide insecticides to all of the south. Malathion was mentioned as its principal product.

Something in the back of his mind began to stir. Something from college chemistry. By the time he reached the office of the Assistant Commercial Attaché, memory had begun to jell. There was something about the chemicals used in insecticides, or fertilizer, that made them useful for other than commercial products.

When he entered the outer office, he was kept at bay by a plump, dark haired, secretary with her hair pinned into a severe French knot. She looked over her half spectacles at Rick, as though he were some kind of unwelcome fungus. Not his usual treatment from ladies.

He wondered where Janine was hanging out. It would be nice to get a look at a friendly face. This commercial guy must be pretty high in rank to rate two secretaries. Janine was certainly a lot more decorative than this one. He was just about to inquire, when the door to the office opened, and Janine, wearing a conservative man-tailored suit welcomed him into her office with a slight smile.

Rick followed her into a modestly furnished office, with the requisite pictures of the President and the Secretary of State the only decorations. There was nothing to indicate any personal life on her desk. There were no photographs of children or husband or dogs. Her manner was equally impersonal this afternoon. She gestured towards a chair near the window, and seated herself behind the government issue, faux mahogany desk. She smiled slightly, as though appreciating his shock, and offered him a cup of coffee from a carafe on her desk. He declined.

"Quite a change from your outfit last evening," he said leaning forward in his chair and looking under the rim of the desk for any electronic gadgets.

She smiled at his routine security check. "The office gets an electronic sweep every morning. We have a special crew that comes in and takes the bugs out, whenever a new cleaning crew puts them in. It's quite a game as you may remember. However, we're never sure that the job is completely done, so you may want to tell me only the essentials of your business here. Do you mind if we have a little music, while we talk?" She switched on a desk top clock radio that began to emit an atonal wailing that would make any conversation difficult to record. She then buzzed the secretary, and asked her to hold all calls. All this was done with a calm efficiency, which was totally different from her manner of the day before.

"You've got this act down pat," he said, standing up and walking around the room. "Now that we are semi-secure, would you mind telling me what part you've got written in this scenario for me. And what assistance, if any, you plan to be in helping me to find my son."

"All in good time, Harrison." She said briskly. "At the moment, I have been instructed to prepare a request for you to accompany Dr. Helmut von Grantz, and his party, into the south. You will go as an observer. It will also give you a chance to see what kinds of fertilizers and pesticides that are being produced in the south. There is a strong possibility, if your mission is successful, that you will be able to make a deal with our Department of Agriculture, and the Tunisian Government, to purchase your company's products to aid in Tunisia's increasingly important agricultural development."

Rick shook his head at the bait being held so blatantly under his nose. But at the same time, he appreciated its economic implications, both to himself and to his company. "Whatever this information is, somebody must want it pretty badly. In economic terms, you are talking millions of dollars in trade for the Tunisians."

He leaned over her desk, his voice low and angry. "But I'm telling you this right now, unless you give me more facts to go on, and some information on my son's whereabouts, I'm going back to Sidi Bou this evening to rip the truth out of an Algerian, who was the last person to see my son."

"I wouldn't try to do that if I were you." She said, walking to the window, and looking out on the bustling street below. "He won't know where Robbie is now any more than you do, or we do for sure. We have tracked the boys to Gafsa, and think that they may be headed toward the Algerian border, perhaps through Tozeur", she added softly.

"But one thing is for sure, if you go barging in to Sidi Bou Said after the Algerian, you may never again see your son alive, since he may be a hostage of these fanatics. These people are enraged, and they think that they are fighting for a holy cause. That often makes them do rather unholy things."

"Then who the hell are they? And what's going on?"

Janine was silent. She was authorized to tell him only so much, but she had a feeling that, unless he knew more, he wouldn't cooperate. She had been told to get his cooperation, but to avoid giving him any classified information. This was one of those decisions on which careers are made or broken. She knew it and she knew she had to take it, because, if she didn't trust Harrison with the basics, it would be practically impossible for him to come up with the information she needed to succeed in her mission. She needed his outsider's expertise, an ex-agent, well versed in toxic chemicals, to do the heavy work on discovering what was going down. She would find out who was behind it, and report back to Washington. It was a career making move

She leaned over toward Rick, keeping her voice low. "For almost a year, we have been tracking increasingly large shipments of substances into the *Magreb*, which, in themselves, are innocent enough, but looked at together have sinister implications for the continuing build up of chemical and nuclear weapons in the Arab world." She lit a cigarette nervously.

"Commercial Attaches' offices were the first to report large shipments of a harmless powder, Dichlor, which can be used to make dyes and insecticides. This was coming into the south of Tunisia. At the same time unusually large quantities of Thiyony Chloride have been shipped to neighboring Algeria."

Rick nodded. "Both of those chemicals are routinely used in pesticides."

"But mixed together," Janine continued, "they make a nerve gas, called Sarin, which is suitable for spraying on human targets from aircraft. It is similar to Malathion, and the list goes on. Even though a large number of precursor materials are now banned for sale to third world countries, there is increasing evidence that Libya is becoming more and more adept at producing these gases from a combination of imported chemicals and those found in their own countries, as has Iraq.

This is what makes Dr. von Grantz's mission of such interest to us. He was involved, according to our sources, in the production of similar substances in East Germany, before the wall came down. She looked at Rick earnestly, her blue eyes somber. "Poison gases are becoming the poor man's atomic bomb. We have to stop these weapons from spreading across Africa and the Middle East."

"You mean they have been tested on the Kurds, and now someone is getting ready to try it on the rest of the countries they don't like?"

"Something like that. And in recent months, the shipments have increased. It looks as though there is a massive build up of these substances that could make Hiroshima look like a rehearsal for doomsday."

Rick was silent for a minute. This was the kind of derry do and save the world that he would have jumped at ten years ago. But now, his bones ached with his desire to find Robbie, and get out of town. Let the world go to hell. It probably deserved it anyhow. He shook his head. "Sounds like a story I've heard before. The good guys and the bad guys slugging it out, while the world's future hangs on the brink."

Janine's eyes grew cold and gray. "But this time your son's life may be on the line. Does that make the job any more interesting?"

Rick restrained an impulse to deck her. Leaving the Assistant Commercial Attaché, or whatever she was, with a black eye, wasn't going to get him any closer to Robbie. And she would probably sue him.

But taking the job that she was offering might help him in the search for his son. And he had no other leads, except the Algerian in Sidi Bou, and that individual probably was no longer there, and if he was, would be unwilling or unable to give Rick any information on where Robbie could be, unless he cut his throat. Which at the moment was a tantalizing possibility.

"Okay, I'll go with von Grantz, if you can provide a suitable cover. But I'm not going to stop looking for Robbie, and if that interferes with the operation, now is the time to call the deal off, and I will refund the airfare."

Janine smiled slightly, for the first time today, looking a little more like the woman he had seen at the party last evening, in her lace earrings. "Harrison, you know, as well as I do, how hard it is to give money back to the government, once it has been spent. We know that you're going to keep looking for Robbie. We believe that he somehow ran afoul of the same right wing religious activists that are involved in the weapons build up. But who they are, and where they are, we don't know. We believe that von Grantz and his party will make contact, while they're in the desert. All you have to do is keep your eyes and ears open and report what you find. We'll do the rest."

"What if I find them first? Who is my backup?"

"Someone will make contact with you in D'Jerba. He is one of our best local operatives. He will stay in touch with you, and let us know if you need help. But please don't try to take things into your own hands. You are there as an observer, nothing more, and if you should do something illegal, you are not on diplomatic or official status, and the Embassy cannot protect you. If anything illegal is being done by the von Grantz group, we will let the Tunisian authorities take care of it." She turned off the radio, and ushered him toward the door.

"The Tunisians are well aware of Robbie's disappearance, and of the transportation of chemicals through their country. They are as anxious to get to the bottom of this as we are. As a matter of fact, they know that their national security may depend on it."

Chapter Four

Harry Olgelvie, the American Ambassador to Tunisia, finished a set of tennis, losing a tie breaker, 6-7 (4-7), and shook hands with Claude Dupont, the French Ambassador, over the net. Both men were out of breath, and wringing wet with perspiration. But neither had been willing to call the game quits before they finished, even though the afternoon sun was at its zenith and the air heavy with humidity.

The ritual game of tennis after lunch was how most of the diplomatic corps worked off the six course dinners that were a part of their evening routine. But Ambassador Olgelvie had something more than tennis on his mind today. He had played hard, but only hard enough to give Dupont a good game, and not to win. He wanted the Frenchman in a good mood today, because he needed information.

In a small country like Tunisia, rumors ran riot and most of the information which was reported back to Washington, had already been talked over, masticated and spit out in almost similar telegrams going pack to London, Paris, Rome and Washington. So Olgelvie was smart enough to check his facts with the French Ambassador. He had received several troubling telegrams from Washington lately asking about a refurbished chemical plant in the south of the country linked to an increase in the imports of possible toxic substances. The issue was delicate, because the Tunisians categorically denied any use of the plant, beyond the development of simple insecticides, pesticides and fertilizer. It might just be true.

Olgelvie mopped his brow with his terry cloth wrist band, and slicked back his gray blonde hair. Later, over a cold glass of lemonade, he broached the subject casually to Dupont.

The results were not helpful, and Olgelvie began to wish that he had won the game. Whatever the Frenchman knew, he was keeping it to himself. He mumbled something about "not taking that kind of talk too seriously, old boy. Besides," he said with a sardonic smile, "if they blow each other up, there's less for us to have to clean up afterwards. Don't forget this is a country of the future, and it always will be. You and I should just serve out our time here, and retire to the Greek islands."

Olgelvie agreed in principle, but he wouldn't give the Frenchman the satisfaction of knowing it. Besides he had to reply to the inquiries from Washington, even just to tell them that they were wrong. He had to get someone down into the country quickly, without alerting the Tunisians and putting their noses out of joint. His people were all too well known, so that left him with this wild card Harrison. Not too reliable from what his people were telling him, and out of the business for awhile. Apt to go off on his own tack. Not exactly a team player. But at the moment, he seemed to be the only player in town.

* * *

The object of this speculation was, at the same time, making his way through the crowded streets of downtown Tunis on foot. He was still angered by his meeting with Janine, and her take it or leave it attitude, which so far, seemed to represent the official position on Robbie, and on the Embassy's conditions for helping to find him. He had, with great difficulty, set up a meeting with the Ambassador for later in the afternoon. The Ambassador's secretary had said that the Embassy's senior diplomat was tied up in an important meeting until three thirty or four, but that Rick could have twenty minutes with him before the close of business at five. Until then, Rick was on his own.

Avenue Bourgiba, the main thoroughfare, was filled with the usual afternoon shoppers. Coffee houses were opening up now, and tables were filling with working men dressed in black pants and white shirts, with here and there, an occasional gelaba. A street vendor moved among them selling peanuts and sweets wrapped in newspaper cones.

Rick was suddenly overcome with a sense of a fatigue. Looking for Robbie, or anyone else, here was like looking for a needle in the proverbial haystack. He caught the wail of Arab music from the omnipresent outdoor speakers. What had tempted Robbie to return here anyhow? What had he expected to find?

He saw a fair haired young man at a far table, and for a moment he thought that it was his son. The boy was about the same build, but as he turned around, Rick saw that he was older and that his hair was bleached, he had no scraggly beard and that his eyes were accented with kohl. From the attention of the men around him, he was glad that it wasn't Robbie.

Rick ordered a coffee, and leaned back in his chair, trying to pretend that he was just another tourist. He had forgotten how much time was just spent, just waiting in the Arab world. It was hard on the nerves. He noticed a young Tunisian, at one of the tables, glancing in his direction, as though he wanted to attract his attention. Rick pointedly ignored his wide eyed stare, but the man was not deterred. Finally, annoyed with the attention, Rick paid his check and walked briskly down the street.

As he turned the corner of a building, he noticed that the young man was following just a few paces behind. His walk was more effeminate than menacing, but his intent to follow was clear. Rick walked more rapidly, and as he neared the entrance to the *Souk*, he ducked behind a vendor with a cart load of cabbages, and a cage full of squawking ducks. He then pretended to be interested in some robes made of cheap, shiny, cotton cloth, and ducked into a store just inside the covered *souk*. The interior was dim and cool, and smelled slightly of sandalwood.

Rick relaxed for a moment, keeping his eye on the doorway. A voice from the interior startled him. It was thin and reedy, but the language was French. "What may I do for you my son? Do you wish to purchase a dress for your wife?" The voice, coming from the back of the store, belonged to an elderly Tunisian gentlemen dressed in a flowing, many colored gelaba, half obscured by the shadows.

He picked a dress off the rack, and held it out for Rick's inspection. Behind him Rick could see the slender, young Arab enter the store. The young Arab pretended to be interested in the clothing, but he never took his eyes off the doorway, as though he were expecting someone to follow. After a few minutes, when no one did, he seemed to relax. He then walked to the back of the store and began to inspect a pile of leather purses. His demeanor had changed. He seemed to be waiting for something, perhaps a chance to speak to Rick.

Rick picked up one of the purses and turned it around in his hands. "It's very careful work," he said in French. "I think my wife would like it."

The young Arab, half turned toward him, showing a thin face with a long scar, like a knife wound down one side of his face. It pulled at the corner of his mouth, giving him an artificial sneer. His eyes were very dark, and almost expressionless.

As Rick moved toward him, the Arab reached for a souvenir dagger hanging on the wall. Whipping the knife out of it's case, he pretended to examine it closely, then without a sound, he moved between Rick and the exit, forcing him at knife point back into the shadows. The pupils of his eyes were large and black showing almost no white, like someone on drugs.

Rick could feel piles of rugs under his feet, and the smell of camel urine used to tan leather was almost overpowering. He backed slowly, feeling the point of the knife at his throat, and cursing himself for being caught so off guard. He was certainly out of practice in this business, or just getting old, or both. The man's smell was acrid, and Rick could feel his breath on his face.

Rick dropped to his knees, catching the Arab off guard for a moment, just long enough to knock the wind out of him with his elbow, and side step the slash of the knife. Rick caught his wrist, and gave it a brutal twist. The man cried out, and dropped the knife soundlessly onto the pile of carpets. The Arab writhed like a cat, rolled over, was on his feet and out the front door before Rick or the old Tunisian could stop him. As he went, he shouted something in Arabic, which caused the old gentleman to recoil, as though he had been struck. He looked at Rick and made a soundless gesture of terror, trying to push him out of the store.

In response to Rick's attempts to question him about this strange, and unexpected encounter, he only shook his head and repeated the word "*An Nahda*," "*An Nahda*". At last almost in desperation, he handed Rick the robe he had been looking at, pushed him out the doorway, and closed the iron grillwork in front of his shop behind him with a resounding clang.

Rick stepped out into the dimly lit *souk*. It was lined on both sides with small shops, exhibiting a variety of colorful goods. The young Arab was nowhere to be seen, and Rick wasn't sure that he wanted to follow, anyway. Dim lit, somber alleyways, lined with shops, stretched off in all directions. Someone, wanting to disappear, would be hard to follow, and almost impossible to catch and identify.

But why had the man followed him? It meant that someone outside of the Embassy was aware of his mission already. Unless the attack was just a random robbery on an unsuspecting tourist. But the man hadn't attempted to steal anything from him. The old Tunisian's fear had been real enough, too.

Rick looked down at the cheap gelaba that the old man had thrust at him. It was the kind that tourists bought to wear over their bathing suits, giving themselves the fun of "going Arab" for a week or two. He rolled it into a ball, and was going to throw it away, but his Scot ancestry stopped him. Instead he tucked it casually under his arm, as he sauntered toward the exit.

He was more cautious now. *An Nahda,* the right wing Arab organization, which had been banned from Tunisian elections, was not to be trifled with. Was this just an attack on an obscure foreign visitor or was it something more sinister?

The narrow walls of the *souk* seemed to press in around him. There were few people in the shops at this hour of the afternoon. Most of the shopkeepers were sitting in the doorways of their stores, having their afternoon coffee. The looks they cast in his direction were only curious, not openly hostile. Yet he began to walk more quickly toward the circle of bright sunlight, that outlined the heavy wooden doorway closed at sunset. In centuries past, he could have been killed for being here, an infidel in an Arab walled town. Now he only watched, out of the corner of his eye, for any suspicious movement from the shadowy shops along his way.

He felt an almost physical sense of relief as he stepped into the sunlight, and hailed a cab to the Embassy. He started to leave the gelaba in the back seat, but decided again to keep it for cover. No one but a tourist would buy such a thing. It was striped brightly in red and purple, with a glittering gold binding around the neck and sleeves. Something that Melanie might have found "amusing" and bought on one of her endless shopping sprees.

As he entered the Embassy, he handed it to the Ambassador's middle-aged secretary. "For your sister in the States," he said, with what he hoped was a disarming smile. The woman simpered, and took it with a look that was decidedly coy and admiring of Rick's rugged good looks. He gained immediate access to Ambassador Olgelvie's office, without the prerequisite ten minutes wait to remind him of the gentleman's importance.

Olgelvie was seated behind a large, black desk, flanked on both sides by the flags of the United States and the Department of State. His face was still slightly flushed by his exertion on the tennis court, but his grip, as he took Rick's hand, was hearty and his demeanor cordial.

"So you're the man I've been hearing so much about." the Ambassador said, offering Rick a drink from a well stocked cabinet. "I've been looking forward to this meeting. We've got ourselves into a position, where none of our regular people can do this little job. Thought you might take it on for us."

"It's a little more complex than that," Rick said, as he laced his drink liberally with soda. "I've only got a few days, a week at most, away from my company, and what is most important, I need your help in locating my seventeen year old son, who is missing somewhere in the *Magreb*."

Olgelvie looked cautious, like a poker player who is holding a full house, and, yet, is trying hard not to give it away. "You have all my sympathy on that one. I have a daughter myself about that age. Amazing the things that they get themselves into these days."

Rick's jaw tightened. "I don't think that you understand me. I'm insisting on Embassy backing in finding Robbie, as a condition for my going along with your scheme to spy on Dr. Whatsis name."

Olgelvie looked shocked. "My dear boy, I'm not asking you to spy on anybody. You're not on our list of covert agents. The Tunisians would be very upset, if they found out that we were sending someone they didn't know down to check out their new agricultural products plant." He took a sip from his glass. "I'm only suggesting that, in your professional capacity as a civilian expert in chemicals, you look out for anything that does not seem to indicate the production of fertilizer or insecticides. In return, you will have our full cooperation in locating your son."

"And if I don't go South?"

"Then we will simply turn the matter of Robbie over to the Tunisian authorities. We know that he was last seen traveling in the company of known drug smugglers."

The Ambassador looked smug. He hadn't felt so good, since he smashed that backhand shot down the line beyond the French Ambassador's reach. He had Harrison where he wanted him now, and for Harrison, there was no turning back.

Rick acknowledged defeat gracefully, despite his anger, but promised himself that his search for his son would be his first priority. His main concern now was for Robbie, and if playing ball with this overfed diplomat was the price for getting him back safely, then so be it.

"When do I leave, and what's my cover?," he asked, briskly moving to the window.

"I believe that Miss Sims has arranged all that. It's my understanding that you will join Dr. von Grantz, and his group, as a commercial observer, in place of our absent Commercial Attaché." He rubbed his plump hands together, playing with his pinkie signet ring with the crest of an eastern school.

"The production plant in Dar el Wadi that you are going to visit was built by our USAID mission a few years ago. It produces commercial fertilizer and insecticides for the south of the country. We believe that some part of it has been converted covertly to produce poison gas. Why, how, and by whom, we don't know."

He paused, looking solemn, "Since I do not have a specialist in such matters on my staff, I asked the Defense Attaché's Office here to procure one for me, informally, so as not to alert or alarm the Tunisians."

"I understand," said Rick, "I'm just to take a quick look, evaluate the situation and report back to you, correct?"

"Yes, and under no circumstances, are you to take any action that would lead the Tunisians to think that we are suspicious of what is going on at Dar El Wadi. If they are in violation of our agreement, that is for our two governments to deal with."

He rose from behind his desk, indicating that the interview was over. "Your role is just that of an informed observer."

"Something like a police dog", Rick said wryly.

The Ambassador nodded, showing him to the door.

"Your travel itinerary will be left in your room at the hotel. Please don't attempt to contact us until you return, except through Miss Sims.

Our telephones are, unfortunately, not always totally secure," he said, as though mentioning halitosis.

As Rick left the room, the Ambassador wiped his brow with a handkerchief, and poured another scotch and soda. Then he called his secretary in to send a "for your eyes only" cable to Washington, informing them of his arrangement of the ex-intelligence agent's visit to Dar el Wadi. He had hooked his quarry and his afternoon's work was finished.

Chapter Five

Rick slept restlessly that night. In his dream, he was searching for Robbie in a *souk* filled with white robed men, who stepped in front of the boy, blocking his way, just as Rick was about to catch up with him. He awoke perspiring, and looked at his watch. It was three a.m.

His instructions had been that he was to join the von Grantz group at the last minute, just as they were leaving town. He was to be a business observer, newly arrived from Washington, as a replacement for the Embassy's Commercial Attaché, who was on home leave. This was to cover his alleged lack of knowledge about the country. He was simply to keep his eyes and ears open, and report on anything unusual that he found at the chemical plant. His instructions listed a number of things that would have been added, if the facility were being used to manufacture something other than insecticides or fertilizers.

He read the instructions that Janine had given him one more time, then carefully tore them in small pieces and flushed them down the toilet.

He lay back down under the thin covers, but sleep wouldn't come. His dream haunted him. It was as though he was searching for Robbie through some kind of maze. It seemed months since he had that initial conversation with Sam in Paris. In reality, it was only three days, and the puzzle kept getting deeper. He felt as though all the people he had contact with at the Embassy were carefully keeping something from him. Surely they knew more about Robbie than they were letting on. He longed to take action, but all his instincts and training told him that he had to go slowly and at least appear to cooperate with the Embassy. He fell into a troubled half sleep.

The telephone rang at five with his wake up call. He rolled over to take it, but the voice on the other end of the telephone wasn't the hotel operator. It was a heavily accented and rasping voice, warning, "Stay out of the south, Monsieur, if you wish to see your son alive. We are watching you. *An Nahda* has eyes everywhere." Then the phone clicked and went suddenly dead. Rick grimaced and swung his lean body out of the bed, hitting the floor in one lithe movement. "The bastards", he muttered as he hurriedly dressed and took the elevator downstairs.

The hotel lobby was empty, except for a lone bellhop, half asleep by the door. There was no desk clerk to be seen, and no one else in the lobby. His attempt to interrogate the bellhop was useless, and a quick glance outside also revealed no one.

The desk clerk appeared languidly behind the desk, but was also ignorant of anyone placing a call to Rick's room. Temporarily defeated, Rick ordered a cup of coffee and a paper in the lobby on the chance that whoever had called him might try to make contact again. He would feel better, knowing what his enemy looked like. By six thirty, the lobby had its share of business men getting ready to leave for flights to Rome and Paris. Most of them were dressed formally and all of them appeared busy with their own affairs. Disgusted and defeated, he decided to return to his room to shower, pack and check out.

As he was about to open door, his nose was assaulted with a strong aroma, almost like almonds. He looked quickly down the hall for it's source. None was evident. He put his key into the keyhole, only to find that the door was already unlocked. His clothes lay strewn all over the floor. His attaché case had been broken open, and even the lining had been slit and torn.

The odor of almonds was almost overwhelming. He walked to the Bath room, and as he opened the door, he was engulfed in a cloud of vapor. Gasping for breath, he grabbed a towel and backed out of the room, covering his nose and mouth with it.

Now his eyes were watering, and he was still trying to get his breath. He backed out of his room and into the hall, slamming the door behind him. He was conscious of the sound of laughter somewhere nearby. He staggered to the end of the hall, and out onto the fire escape, filling his lungs with great gulps of fresh air. He was covered with perspiration, and his hands were shaking. Whoever these people were, they were serious, and had warned him again, this time the hard way.

He felt nauseous, and close to passing out as he staggered out side. He knew how to play rough too and it looked as if he was going to do just that. This morning had only convinced him that someone was playing for keeps, and whatever game *An Nahda* was up to, he would have to beat them at their game if he were to survive.

He decided to avoid calling the police, who would only question him and delay his mission. He wanted to get out of the hotel, with as little fuss as possible. Whoever these people were, he didn't want them to know that he was concerned by their warning. He hastily paid his bill and hurried to the appointed meeting place by the Embassy, stopping to purchase an expensive new attaché case on the way. He had the feeling that he was being followed, but the streets were crowded now with young men wearing gelabas, and it was hard to tell one from another.

He found a Land Rover parked in front of the Embassy compound with Dr. von Grantz, and his group, waiting impatiently. Rick glanced at his watch. It was still five minutes before the appointed meeting time, but apparently not early enough for the Germans. He murmured an apology, as he introduced himself as a last minute replacement for the absent Commercial Attaché. Dr. von Grantz was evidently not pleased with this substitution, but he barked an order to the driver and the Land Rover rolled forward though the early morning traffic.

Fortunately the motor made so much noise that conversation was almost impossible. Rick was packed between a rather plump young

German with ice blue eyes, and a well built, silent Tunisian. Dr. von Grantz rode in front with the driver, attempting to converse with him in heavily accented French. The Arab driver either didn't understand, or pretended not to. Rick decided that it was going to be a long trip.

*   *   *

Sam smiled, as he pulled the message from Tunis off the fax. So his boy was going to deliver after all. He had had a few bad moments after Olgelvie's first message, but he thought he knew Rick. Rick was as tenacious as a bull dog, once he had taken an assignment. The trick was to get him interested enough to want to be involved again. He had been completely burnt out ten years ago, but once an intelligence type, always a player. They couldn't burn that out of you. Sam ran his fingers through his thinning hair as he put the document from Olgelvie through the shredder.

But where in the hell was Robbie? Someone should have had a line on him by now. Tunisia was a small country. And with all the people in the field, it was odd that no one had turned up a real lead on his whereabouts. The trail, as he knew it from Paris, ended in Sidi Bou Said. He only hoped that Rick didn't find his son dead somewhere in the desert. He sighed and shook his head. This was a nasty business he had chosen for a career. He only hoped that this last assignment worked out for both Rick and himself. If not, Rick would be dead, and he might as well be.

*   *   *

Rick narrowed his eyes against the sun. The Land Rover had long since turned off of the paved road. They were now traveling over what could only be described as a track through the desert. Dr. von Grantz had ceased his unsuccessful attempts to converse with the driver, and the whole party had fallen into a half stupor, caused by the rocking of the vehicle, and the fine brown dust permeating the air.

Lunch was eaten from a hamper, in back of the Land Rover. The Germans talked quietly, and the Arabs ignored each other. Dr. von Grantz seemed to have accepted Rick's cover story, and he seemed only anxious about reaching Dar El Wadi before nightfall. He kept drinking water, thirstily, from the tank carried on the back of the Land Rover, until the Tunisian member of the group, warned him that there was still a long way to go, and that was all the water they carried.

After lunch, the party cheered up a bit, and, over hot sweet cups of tea, prepared by the driver, the tall, dark eyed, Tunisian introduced himself. He was Ahmed Haddad, an army officer, on detail to assist the German team in their inspection of Dar El Wadi. Rick smiled to himself, translating "assist", to "keep a sharp eye on the foreigners and see what they are up to."

He felt a sort of comradeship for the man. If he only knew it, they were both here on the same assignment. The only question was, were they both on the same side? In this instance, Rick rather doubted it. Whatever was going on at Dar El Wadi, had to be with the knowledge of some high level Tunisians, probably the military, or someone from the outside working with them. This country was too tightly controlled for much to be going on here that the military didn't know about.

About sundown, they reached a small town, which rose up out of the desert to greet them, as though created completely from the sand. All the houses were made of brown clay, and the one small hotel, looked like something out of a western movie. In the distance, he could make out the looming hulk of the chemical plant, with the sun setting behind it. It looked amazingly large and complex for this part of the world. Huge, shining storage tanks reflected the last glowing light from the sun. But the area seemed deserted, like something on the moon.

His fellow passengers stumbled into the small hotel, complaining loudly about the dust and the heat. Rick was amused that he still understood so much German. Dr.von Grantz seemed a strange one to have been sent on an assignment like this. So far, his only concern seemed to be for water to drink or to wash in. He had a habit of continually rubbing his hands together, as though trying to get them clean under an imaginary faucet. At the same time, he spoke to his pie faced colleague, Hanz, in a high pitched, nasal voice. Rick had to resist an impulse to reach out, and shut off the imaginary flow of water.

The innkeeper greeted them at the door with much bowing, and many protestations about how happy he was to have them in his humble abode. His long gelaba was stained at the hem from dragging on the floor, and he had the hawk nosed profile of a man of the desert. He waved them into the shabby entrance of his inn, as though he were welcoming them to the Ritz. The Germans made several uncomplimentary remarks in their native tongue, and then began to demand beer and something to eat.

Rick excused himself from the group, saying that he needed to stretch his legs. He wanted to go outside before it became completely dark to get the lay of the land towards the "fertilizer plant", or whatever the Tunisians wanted to call it. If possible, he wanted to take a look at it tonight, before the official visit in the morning. In the fading light of the sun, the plant looked deserted. High barbed wire fences surrounded the grounds, looking incongruous in this desert landscape. There was one main gate, also topped with barbed wire, protected by a lone man, slumped against the guard shack, looking half asleep.

The fence itself didn't look as if it would be hard to climb. The barbed wire looked less than vicious in this light, and could be covered with a blanket to avoid any injury. He strolled closer, ignoring the ragged children who pursued him curiously. Finally he threw them a handful of coins to get rid of them, so that he could continue his solitary stroll. A voice behind him said angrily, "Do not teach our children to beg." It was Ahmed, the Tunisian military officer, freshly washed and brushed. He looked Rick over curiously, his brown eyes hard under his straight, black eyebrows.

Rick smiled and offered him a cigarette, to defuse the moment. "No offense meant," he said lightly. "All small boys like money."

The officer took the cigarette and tapped it lightly on the back of his hand. "Everyone likes money", he said, with his eyes narrowed. "It is what they do to get it, that shames us all."

Rick nodded, again feeling a sense of comradeship for the man. "That is true in my country as well", he said, grinding out his cigarette in the sand.

Ahmed smiled with a certain bitterness. "But here, as you can see", he said, waving his arm toward the desert, "there is not so much to steal."

"Only for those who prize fertilizer", Rick replied, and moved slightly forward as though to continue his stroll toward the fertilizer plant. The officer moved forward with him, and put a restraining hand on his arm.

"Perhaps we should join the others", he said, "This area is not safe after dark. Too many petty thieves in this village, who prey on tourists."

Rick nodded, promising himself to continue his walk later, after dark.

After the communal dinner, provided by the inn keeper for the group, Rick lay in his bed, waiting for the sounds of the inn to quiet down, assuring him that everyone was asleep. The dinner of mutton and cous cous had been heavy enough, and copious enough, to assure everyone of a sound night's sleep. He had been amazed at the Germans capacity to eat and drink. He could hear Dr. von Grantz snoring soundly in the next room. Finally, Rick decided to wait no longer. Apparently everyone was asleep and his nocturnal wanderings would go unnoticed.

He slipped out of bed, and padded to the window in his stocking feet. Outside there was just a wisp of a moon, lending a surreal light to the landscape. The street looked deserted, and his digital watch read three a.m. He slipped on tennis shoes with his dark pants and sweater, and made his way stealthily out of the room, and down the stairs. He paused by the doorway, hearing a sound, but it was only someone calling out in his sleep. He opened the door softly, and slipped into the street. The air felt cold and fresh after the enforced waiting in his stuffy room. He could still feel the heavy mutton dinner in his stomach.

The moon cast long shadows across the street. Rick was able to make his way by staying close to buildings and moving swiftly across the distances which divided them. He was close to the plant's fence now. He examined it carefully for alarms and found nothing obvious. At the same time, the wind came up blowing the sand at his feet and scattering small pebbles behind him. He tossed one of the larger pebbles at the fence. There was no reaction. Rick assumed it was probably not wired.

When he put a hand on the chain link fence, though, he was rewarded by a strong, electric shock. Apparently, someone was concerned enough to make sure that there were no unexpected visitors to Dar El Wadi. He circled the fence cautiously, looking for a break, or a place where he could wiggle through. Finally, he found a shallow depression in the sand, which looked as though careless workmen had fenced over a small *wadi*, or stream bed, without filling it in, or perhaps the recent rains had washed it out again. More likely, the latter. Rick marked it mentally.

Even in the moonlight, he could tell that it was a large operation. Much more extensive than an ordinary insecticide or fertilizer plant. There were a series of buildings, which looked like huge sheds used for storage and acres of out buildings. All of it looked incongruous here in the middle of the desert. Rick began to feel that Sam's suspicions were probably not unfounded.

He tripped over a long wire stretched taut to support the fence poles. The noise seemed to echo across the desert, setting up vibrations that reached to the hills. He froze, hearing distant voices. The voices came nearer. Rick flattened himself against the ground. He held his breath, cursing his clumsiness. The voices were speaking in Arabic, and they sounded conversational, rather than alarmed. Rick rolled over, lowering himself into the shallow *wadi*. The smell of sand was in his nostrils, and in his mouth, as he tried to become invisible to the newcomers. He lay still for what seemed like an eternity, barely breathing.

The sounds stopped. He wriggled forward in the crevice, and felt the top of his head hitting barbed wire on the bottom of the fence. Pulling his chin in, he inched forward, feeling the barbed wire scrape along his back. Fortunately, the barbed wire itself didn't seem to be electrified, or connected to the alarm system.

In a few moments, he was through. He crouched in the half-moonlight, waiting. But the desert was silent. The guards had moved on out of earshot. He moved cautiously along the perimeter of the fence, mentally marking the spot where he had entered, so he could exit quickly.

In the moonlight the vast chemical storage bins rose to his right, like conical hills. To his left, long low buildings disappeared into the shadows. There wasn't a glimmer of light anywhere. It looked like most chemical plants he had seen, except for the excessive number of storage tanks. Hard to believe that a country as small as Tunisia could use all of that insecticide or fertilizer that could be stored in these tanks.

He edged nearer the tanks, moving at a half crouch to avoid being seen by the gate guard. Once in their shadow, he flattened himself against the cool, metal side, edging around the circumference of it with the metal at his back. He was aware of a peculiar acrid odor, somehow familiar.

The sound of voices coming nearer, caused him to drop to the ground. Sleepy Arab voices, seemingly in conversation, gave no hint of alarm. They passed close to him, one of the men stopping for a moment to light a cigarette. Certainly a forbidden pleasure, with all of these chemicals around. He could see the flare of the match out of the corner of his eye. These men were either the changing of the guard, or additional perimeter security.

The man laughed and repeated a word to his companion, which sounded like "hash ", then *"kief kief"*, he repeated in Arabic, and laughed again. Rick willed himself to stop breathing, until they left.

The overly sweet smell of marijuana filled the night air, masking the acrid odor of the something else that was troubling familiar. A scent, like almonds, seemed to be coming from the iron tanks behind him, or perhaps it was coming from some residue of the chemical, saturating the ground. It was not a smell associated with the chemical products he knew.

He listened as the voices faded into the night, then, taking advantage of a moment when the moon was obscured behind a cloud, he made his way cautiously back to the fence and his escape route without attracting attention.

The small hotel was still black. And not even a dog prowled the silent streets. Whoever was running this operation, if it was clandestine, must not have any great fear of being discovered security was so light. He eased himself up the stairs, and back into his quiet bedroom. As he opened the door, he caught the scent of jasmine. A hand covered his mouth and he felt the cold, hard steel of a pistol pressed into his ribs. The door closed silently behind him. He heard the key reinserted in the lock and turned.

A warm, female form pushed against him, with the gun still lodged firmly into his ribs. Soft lips brushed against his ear, and a husky voice murmured, "Don't resist, and nothing fatal will happen to you. Why don't you begin by telling me why you're in my room?"

Chapter Six

With a panther-like movement Rick turned and faced the woman, pulling her roughly against him. He could hear her laugh softly as she yielded to him, her body fitting itself to his. He could feel himself responding, awakening to her familiar scent and to his need.

Rick backed away from the door, with his arm around the woman's waist. With his left hand, he reached for a small light near the bed. By its dim glow, he recognized Janine. She was wearing jeans and her hair pulled back in a tight pony tail, but the gun in her hand looked like business. She watched him with a tantalizing smile, as she slowly tucked it into the front of her jeans.

"Sorry," she said, pulling the clip out of her blond hair and shaking it loose with her free hand." I knew that you were gone, and I didn't know who else might be coming into your room in the middle of the night. We heard about the attack on you in Tunis after you left. The boss thought that you might need some backup."

"Then you agree that it is my room," Rick said, with an edge to his voice. "Would you mind telling me what you're doing here in the middle of the night."

"Change of plans," she said huskily. "The boss thinks that they may be on to you, so I'm here to provide additional cover and perhaps confuse them a little bit about what you're doing."

"This is a dandy way to start."

"Couldn't be helped. It will all be very official in the morning," she said, leaning towards him. "Von Grantz isn't as stupid as he looks, and the Tunisian covering him is a high ranking officer of the government's elite army guard. The boss says to tread very carefully." Janine settled back on the bed comfortably. " The whole project seems to be further along than we thought and to involve some rather high level people."

"Well, I can tell you one thing. They are making more than fertilizer out there. Fertilizer may be one of the bi-products, but there is probably enough poison gas in a couple of those tanks to wipe out half the population of Tunis, and who knows what is in the rest of them."

"Are you sure?"

"Sure enough not to want to step inside one."

Janine sat up, and rubbed her face wearily. "Then you're in more danger than I thought. Maybe we both are. But all we can do now is to play the game tomorrow of looking like innocent Embassy observers. I've got to get a message out immediately to our man in D'Jerba without arousing suspicion."

"And just how do you plan to do that? There's only one phone and it's on the desk in the hall. This is hardly the time to call home to mother."

Janine rolled over on her stomach and pulled a small cellular phone out of her copious leather purse. She smiled at him impishly in the dim light. "ET phone home", she said, punching in a number.

"Good, and while you do that, I'm going to get a little sleep. Do you want to stay here, or do you actually have a room in this flea bag?"

"Don't you like these first class, Embassy accommodations? Anyway, not to worry," she said over the top of the phone, "I booked myself the room next door."

Rick muttered something under his breath, rolled over and, before he knew it, was almost asleep. He could still hear Janine's voice talking to her "mother" about how much wind there was in the desert. "Sure is a lot of hot air," he thought, as drifted toward sleep, still aware of her scent, jasmine and woman mixed in a tantalizing fashion.

He was awakened by the touch of a warm hand on his back. He flipped over, ready to kill. The lips that touched his were warm and eager, and smelled slightly of jasmine. There were no words, only passion activated by danger and mutual need.

Janine's body was thin and as supple as a teenager's, but her hands and mouth were that of an experienced woman. Rick breathed her in, and allowed himself to be seduced, and then seduced her in return. She stifled her cries against his shoulder when she came in an explosion of delight. Then she urged him on to explore her again, more and more deeply, until he peaked, hung suspended for a moment, and climaxed.

When it was finally over, she lay beside him for a moment, languidly tracing his belly with the tips of her fingers. Then she was gone. Rick fell into a deep and dreamless sleep

*   *   *

Robbie stirred uncomfortably in his sleep. He had been dreaming that he was home in Bethesda with mom and dad. He was little again, and he kept telling them that he was afraid and that he was lost, but they couldn't hear him. He woke up with his throat dry, his head hurt and his legs were numb from being tied. For a moment, he thought that perhaps this was the dream, and that in a second or two, he would wake up in his own bed in his house on Jackson street. He heard a sound, and realized that he was sobbing, loud angry sobs in the dark. But no one came. He was alone.

*   *   *

Rick woke to the sun stabbing through his window, like shards of broken glass. His eyes felt like someone had been rubbing sand into them, and his throat was dry. The connecting door to Janine's room was locked, and all evidence of her nocturnal visit had vanished.

He glanced at his watch, and realized that it was almost time to make the official inspection of the "fertilizer" plant.

There was a discrete knock at the door. At his mumbled permission, the door opened, and a slender Arab boy, of almost breathtaking beauty, entered bearing a tray with tea and hot bread. "Missy send me," he said quietly, nodding toward the closed door. His eyes were large and dark, and scanned the room, missing nothing. "You, American man, you need anything you let Mohammed know."

Rick grimaced at the suggestion, and waved the boy away, with what he hoped was a smile. "Just tea for now, thank you, and perhaps some hot water to shave in."

"I bring for you," the boy answered, with a beatific smile, and before Rick could say more, he had fled the room, to return in a few minutes with a basin of hot water, smelling of orange blossoms. He stood near the door waiting, as Rick shaved, his huge eyes taking in every motion of the razor. Rick had no more luck getting rid of him, than he would have of a puppy. Finally he handed him the basin of soapy water and asked him to leave, sweetening the command with a few coins. The boy obeyed reluctantly, finally backing out of the room, as though he were in the presence of royalty.

When Rick came downstairs a few minutes later, the Germans were already standing together outside the front door, waiting for their vehicle. They were dressed in matching Abercrombie and Fitch desert outfits: shorts, belted jackets and knee socks topped off with wide brimmed khaki hats. Hanz's shorts were a bit tight for his fat bottom and he kept tugging at them surreptitiously. There was no sign of Janine, and Rick began to wonder again about their late night encounter. The Tunisian officer was there, heavy lidded and correctly uniformed. He stood apart from the group looking towards the hotel, as though expecting someone.

That someone apparently was Janine. She came through the door of the hotel dressed in a beige cotton suit, and carrying a large black attaché case. Her hair was pulled back in a bun, and she looked the model of female Foreign Service Officer. The Tunisian officer bowed slightly and shook her hand, while she told him her cover story, loud enough for the Germans to overhear. She nodded at Rick, giving him a cool eyed glance that belied recognition, as she climbed into the Land Rover ahead of him.

The drive to the fertilizer plant took only a few minutes. The Land Rover entered by the main gate, on the opposite side from the large storage tanks, and stopped in front of some of the low roofed buildings, that Rick had observed the night before. The group was met at the door by the Director General of the Dar el Wadi operation, a small Tunisian of indeterminate age and of little English.

He led them to his office, and as a usual sign of Arab courtesy, offered them all hot, sweet cups of coffee. The Germans, bored by the delay and wanting to get started, refused. Janine and the Tunisian officer saved the day by politely accepting the ritual offering.

It was soon apparent that much of the tour was to be of these outbuildings. Try as he would, Rick was not able to get as near to any of the storage tanks as he had the night before. Janine was having no better luck, as the Tunisian officer dogged her steps even to the door of the ladies' room.

By the end of the morning, they were all hot and tired and little had been accomplished, except to have visited all of the outbuildings and listened to a very detailed explanation of the workings of the plant. Rick's only consolation was that the Germans were even more uncomfortable, and disappointed. Dr. von Grantz seemed to forget most of his English and conversed with his aide only in German, which began to sound more and more agitated. Finally, after being shown another of the low buildings, stacked to the ceiling with empty fertilizer bags, the group agreed to return to the hotel for lunch.

"Boring, boring, boring," Janine whispered, as they climbed the stairs to their respective rooms, to wash away the dust before lunch. "Whatever is going on here is in deep, deep cover."

"I think Haddad has eyes for you," Rick said, grimly, "He hasn't taken his eyes off you all morning. But then neither have I."

"He's probably just interested in the contents of my attaché case," she said, smiling wickedly. "Anyhow, there will be reinforcements waiting for us at D'Jerba, if we make it that far."

Before Rick could answer, the door to von Grantz's room opened, and he came out, freshly washed and looking grim. He bowed stiffly toward Janine. "A pleasure to have you join us, Miss Sims", he said, stiffly." I didn't think that our little tour was of such interest to your government. Have you learned much this morning?"

Janine feigned polite boredom, "Nothing that the Tunisians haven't already informed us of," she said levelly. "But it's always interesting to see these agricultural projects first hand. What was your impression Dr. von Grantz?"

"I was disappointed with the level of production," he said, his sibilants hissing like a rattlesnake. "Perhaps D'Jerba will be better."

"Yes, I have instructions to accompany you and Dr. Harrison there", Janine said smoothly. "The Ambassador is most interested to have first hand knowledge of the development of the D'Jerba plant."

Rick winced inwardly at the use of his academic title. He knew that she was doing it to put the German in his place. But he doubted the wisdom of the tactic, right at this moment.

"Ah yes, Dr. Harrison", the German said, turning his cold gray eyes on Rick. "And what is your impression of what we have seen this morning?"

"Hard to tell without a more complete tour of the facility", Rick said jovially. "I imagine we can look forward to that this afternoon."

"That is difficult to say", the German replied. "The Tunisians are somewhat touchy about the state of their technology. We have probably seen all that we will be allowed to see here. I shall personally meet with them again, this afternoon before we leave."

Rick glanced at Janine. And check all the formulas, he added mentally, and probably take a few samples. If, as Rick believed, the German was indirectly responsible for the deaths of thousands of Kurds with the use of poison gasses, he would put his hands around the German's scrawny throat and squeeze it tightly, just for the sheer satisfaction of having von Grantz gasp for breath, and beg for mercy, as the Kurds had done.

The German stiffened, as though reading his thoughts. "Shall ve haff lunch?", he said, preceding them down the stairs.

*   *   *

It was many hours earlier in Washington, D.C., and Melanie Weston held the telephone receiver clutched angrily in her beautifully manicured right hand, while, with her left, she turned the pages of the Washington Post. She had been put on hold by the Embassy operator in Tunis. Melanie was not used to being kept waiting, and did not like it at all.

The only daughter of a wealthy industrialist who manipulated politics by backing Congressional candidates who could cast a deciding vote for his industry when necessary, Melanie was used to having things her own way. Having Rick unavailable when she wanted him, was making her very cross. And when Melanie was cross, everyone heard about it.

Slamming down the receiver on the long distance call, she placed another to Sam Shepherd's office at the Embassy in Paris. When his secretary said that he was unavailable, too, she fumed, and dialed her father immediately, taking the portable phone out onto the veranda.

She liked her Georgian townhouse in Washington's Foggy Bottom. It certainly was better than the house that she and Rick had owned in Bethesda. The townhouse was large enough to entertain, and small enough to be just right for the intimate dinner parties she gave when her father was in town. These parties connected all the right people at the right time, before important decisions affecting her father's wide spread commercial interests were made in Congress.

She pushed back her auburn hair, with an immaculately groomed, small hand. Her skin was pale and almost translucent, and her blue eyes, round and guileless, like a little girl's. "The iron butterfly", her father liked to call her. People who got in her way had been known to call her other less flattering names. Since her divorce from Rick ten years ago, she had had a series of escorts, but no serious romances. Rumor had it, that under her melting glances, she was as cold as ice. The only lover that seemed to permanently attract her was power.

But now she was frightened. Robbie was missing, and he was the one thing in the world that she feared losing. He was her prime achievement, her token to show the world that she was successful after all. And now someone, or something, was trying to take him from her.

When her father's private line was busy, she redialed the Embassy in Tunis. This time, she was told that all the circuits were busy. She kept hitting the redial button over and over, frantically, until her finger was almost numb. Finally, in desperation, she called Air France, and booked a first class seat on the evening flight to Paris. At least there, she might be able to get hold of Sam Shepherd in person, and she would only be a few hours away from Tunisia. The waiting would be less agonizing, since she would be doing something positive about finding Robbie, and besides, she could see the couturiers fall fashion collections.

Now that she knew that she was about to go after Robbie, she tried her father's number again. When Duke answered, Melanie told him of her plans, and that she would keep him informed of her whereabouts and her progress. She also asked for a large increase in her monthly allowance to cover her expenses in Paris.

*   *   *

Duke Weston, sitting in his 26th floor office in New York, put down the phone after talking to his daughter, and stared out the window at the empire that oil leases, access to other natural resources and contacts in Washington had built. He was a big man, with thick, white hair, and a torso that seemed too large for the rest of his body. He knew that Melanie had spoiled his grandson, and babied him, until he had become a whiner and a sissy.

He had hoped that traveling alone this summer would put some starch in Robbie. Instead, he had gotten himself lost or in trouble. But at least the dreaded ransom note, or call hadn't yet come. It was as if Robbie had dropped off the face of the earth and in Tunisia of all places.

Duke hoisted himself out of his chair and went to one of the side walls of his office, covered from ceiling to floor with a concealed map of the world, showing all of the Weston enterprises. Tunisia was empty of markers, as were most of its neighbors. The projects that were underway in those countries, were highly confidential and remained unmarked on the map. These "special" projects were done under the auspices of a corporation that in no way could be linked to Weston Enterprises.

But now Robbie was out there, lost, or worse still, being held for ransom of some kind. At any rate, he was now an unknown factor to Duke Weston in an international game as well as Duke's only grandson and heir. Duke had made his fortune by always betting on sure things. Robbie's disappearance was highly disturbing. It didn't fit this scenario.

He would give his former son-in-law, Rick Harrison, just three more days to find his son, Robbie, before he began to twist some arms himself, even though he knew that the results might not be pretty. He pushed a button, concealing the map of the world, and placed a call to Washington.

* * *

Ambassador Olgelvie studied the telegrams on his desk. There was no mention of the missing Harrison boy, but there was a decided note of urgency in the communiqués that he was getting from the "other" agency. There was nothing from Harrison, or Janine Sims, not that he had expected anything, yet. It wasn't his idea to send Harrison anyhow, and it was highly irregular, using a non-governmental individual on a sensitive task, like this one. He dictated a memo to the file, which cleared him of all responsibility, should things go wrong in the south.

He then called the French Ambassador, and booked a game of tennis for right after lunch. A bit of fresh air always cleared the brain. Besides, Janine was capable of looking after Harrison, and of keeping him on track, or at least out of the hands of the Tunisian secret service. She was a smart woman, sharp as a tack. Too bad she was a member of the "other" agency, and not a part of the regular Foreign Service. She would have made a good Commercial Attaché.

He glanced again at the reports covering his desk. The Tunisians had more than doubled their exports of potassium in the last months, and at the same time had opened another new fertilizer plant in the south. That would mean that they would not depend so heavily on American imports. Good for the Tunisians, but bad for the American balance of trade.

He leafed through the day's invitations. Cocktails with the Germans, dinner with the French and a late night coffee with the Egyptians. He buzzed his secretary, and asked her to arrange a lunch with the Minister of Agriculture. The tennis match would help after a big Tunisian lunch.

*   *   *

Janine put down her fork, and stared out of the window. One of the hardest parts of her job was the continual eating. Not that she didn't like food, but eating was such a ritual in Tunisia, and particularly on a mission such as this one. She watched the Germans attack their food. Dr. von Grantz ate like a machine, never changing expression, but chewing every bite thoroughly as though it were his duty. Conversation was limited. The Tunisian officer, Ahmed, was unfailingly polite, but he watched her constantly, his eyes half closed as though he were memorizing her every movement.

She had been unable to contact D'Jerba a second time. It was imperative that they get some backup by the time they got there. Harrison didn't seem as sharp as she had been led to believe. Or maybe it was just the ten years out of the business. Perhaps he had just gotten soft, used to making money, and not taking chances. She wondered if he wouldn't be able to handle it if things got really rough. The way the Tunisian was watching her, it was possible that they were riding straight into an ambush.

Headquarters had been very vague about what they were to expect at Dar el Wadi and D'Jerba. It was certain that the island of D'Jerba would be full of tourists this time of year. But that was always an excellent cover for clandestine activities. Almost anyone could come and go with a tour group from Germany or France, and never be noticed. D'Jerba had become a mecca for anyone wanting to pick up a winter tan, and perhaps a small amount of hash, continuing the islands legendary history of the site where Ulysses was detained on his way back from Troy, in the land of the Lotus eaters. For traffickers, it also was easily approachable from air and sea.

She looked up and saw von Grantz watching her warily. He had sharp pointed incisors, that made him look like a hunting dog, and when he spoke English, he revealed them as he struggled for correct pronunciation.

"Will you be accompanying us to D'Jerba, *gnadiga frau*? Are you able to take so much time from your important work at the Embassy?," He hissed at her across the table. As he spoke, spittle formed at the corners of his mouth, reminding Janine of a rabid dog she had once seen in the streets of Tunis.

Being called a graceful lady in German didn't increase her liking for him, so she answered him in correct German, just to take some of the wind out of his sails. "The Ambassador is anxious that I do everything I can to make your trip a success, Dr. von Grantz. He has asked me to stay with you, to assure him that the trip is going smoothly."

Von Grantz looked as startled as his expressionless face would allow. "But you speak excellent German, where did you learn it?"

Janine saw Rick watching her from across the table. "At the university," she lied gracefully, looking down at her well filled plate.

Later, when they went upstairs to their rooms, Rick knocked and then pushed open the door to their adjoining rooms. Janine was sitting on the bed, seemingly deep in thought. Her briefcase was open on the bed beside her. She looked up as Rick entered, and hastily pushed some papers back into the case and closed it abruptly.

"I thought that we were supposed to be working together? What's the point of letting von Grantz know that you understand German? That's just makes it easier for their side."

She looked at him, languidly, her chameleon like face changing from hard nosed professional, surprised innocence. "I guess I just lost it for a minute. I just wanted to put him in his place."

"One of the first rules I learned in this business, was that you have to try to keep personal feelings out of things. It's the very best way to trip up yourself and your colleagues as well. What do you hear from D'Jerba?"

"I got through once, but now no one is picking up the transmission, or at least they're not answering. We're on our own anyhow for the next two days. I can stay with the group, if you want to go on ahead."

"And do what?", Rick answered angrily. "I'm no closer to finding my son than I was four days ago in Paris, and my time is running out. I expect some help from your people, and it's about time you begin to deliver. Otherwise I'm going to the Tunisians directly."

"I wouldn't do that if I were you. There is an American girl who has been in jail here for a year, who was caught bringing only two ounces of hash across the border. My sources tell me that Robbie and his friends had a great deal more than that."

"Then, if you know so much, where in the hell is he?" Rick asked, grabbing her by the arm, and pulling her to him harshly.

She resisted initially, and then sank against his chest with a muffled cry as he held her arm behind her back. "I told you. I don't know exactly, but we think that he is maybe near one of the oases in the south. It seems he was picked up by some camel drivers and then traded to another group of Bedouins, but we don't know why or exactly where they're holding him. Damn it, will you stop twisting my arm?," she said, trying to pull away. "As you said, we're supposed to be on the same side."

"That's what I thought too", Rick said grimly, "but maybe if I twist your arm a little harder, you'll remember at near which oasis they're supposed to be holding my son."

Her face was turning white with anger, as well as with pain, and her mouth was set in a grim line that Rick had seen before. If she knew where Robbie was now, she wasn't going to tell him yet. Slowly he released the pressure, and pulled her against him, holding her lightly, as if in a caress, remembering their night together. "I'm sorry to have hurt you, but I'm really desperate to find Robbie and you have information that I don't have. You've got to help me. I've got so little time, and what I do have is running out rapidly."

She looked up at him, her eyes narrow and hard. "You bastard. Do you think I'd fall for the oldest trick in the book, that lovey dovey stuff. Last night is one thing, but we're both professionals, and when we get to D'Jerba, and I'm free to do so, I'll tell you what I know. Until then, you'll either have to kill me, or be patient."

Rick touched her face, trying to awaken a memory of their passion.

She pulled away from him angrily." I don't know where your damn son is and if I did I wouldn't tell you. Why don't you just take off and look for him if you're in such a hurry. I can look after myself. I don't need you or anyone else to help me."

Rick backed away from her. His eyes narrowed. " You better be prepared to watch your back lady, because I may do just that tomorrow morning."

Chapter Seven

The group that climbed into the Land Rover the next morning, was almost beyond being civil to each other. Dr. von Grantz announced that he wanted to take a slight detour, to inspect the sites where potassium was mined near Gafsa, a detour which would cost them the better part of a day.

Rick started to protest, but then, looking at Janine, decided against it. Von Grantz was clearly a man under orders, and it suited whoever was running him to have the whole group arrive in D'Jerba almost a day late.

Apparently, they were being kept out of town for a reason, a reason that he had to find out as soon as possible. Getting away from the group was his only chance. Janine would have to take her chances with the group alone. From the look of her, she was used to doing just that.

Rick put on his most indignant, American businessman voice. "But Grantz, look here. I've got appointments in D'Jerba. The American Embassy in Tunis borrowed me from my company, and it won't put up with any more delay. I've got to get back to Paris next week with a full report, or they'll have my job." This part at least was true.

Von Grantz looked at him through slightly hooded eyes. He licked his lips with the tip of his tongue. "Then, perhaps my friend, you should leave us and go on ahead. We can meet you in D'Jerba day after tomorrow at the hotel we have selected, and you can return with us to Tunis, when we have completed our mission there."

Rick, despite the look of caution Janine gave him, seized the opportunity. "Sure, tell me where you're staying and I'll meet you there. I can take off cross country and save some time."

Which is how Rick found himself, a few hours later in an old, rented Jeep, driving across some of the roughest roads he had ever been on, straight towards the desert and the oasis of Tozeur. He had a sense of lightness and freedom, as he sped along the dusty roads. For the first time since he started this journey, he had the feeling that he was his own master, and not just a puppet being jerked around by Sam and his kind.

It certainly looked as if somebody was busy making poison gasses, of one kind or another, in this country. He was now sure of that, even though he didn't know which. He also could make an educated guess, based upon the current world situation, and particularly here in the *Magreb*, who their customers might be. That was essentially all that Sam had asked him to find out, and it was time that he worked full time on the rest of the puzzle, Robbie's whereabouts.

He remembered Robbie as a sturdy four year old, and then as a first grader, eager for school. After the divorce, Robbie had grown more and more distant, probably from listening to Melanie's complaints about his father, until, in these last years, he had become a rangy, slightly sullen, teenager, verging on young manhood. Rick had no idea of what was in his mind or why he would have made this journey alone this summer. He felt a surge of anger at Melanie for letting him go.

Whatever the kid had gotten himself into, it wasn't pretty. If what Janine was implying was true, he'd be lucky to get out of the country without serving a term in jail for possession or worse.

Rick drove with one hand, while he tried to consult the map out of the corner of his eye. The road stretched before him as straight as a string, and the country looked like the panhandle of Texas, without the cows. As far as he could see, there was nothing but flat, brown land, and a rising haze of dust, kicked up by the tires of his jeep. The hardest part of the drive to Tozeur was just staying awake.

Later in the afternoon as, as he got closer to the desert, the landscape began to change into shimmering heat pictures, painting themselves across his mind. He stopped the jeep, and drank deeply of his water supply, even expending some of it on the back of his neck.

After a while, the heat images vanished but, stretching out on either side of him, was a landscape that reminded him of photographs of the moon. He was on the edge of the Chott el Jerid, an immense saltpan, covering almost 3000 square miles. The road to Tozeur ran through it, on a man made causeway, raised above its surface, which was dry and blistered like burned flesh.

Here and there, puddles of water remained, reflecting pink and green, as the light shimmered above them. A few souvenir stands began to dot the road, and Rick stopped at one of them, to ask directions.

He pretended interest in a rug, and the proprietor was upon him like a spider on a fly. But a spider eager to show his wares. Rick bargained half-heartedly, finding out that the man was originally from this region, but now returned only during the *bonne saison*, to sell his rugs, and the succulent dates, which were harvested this time of year. Rick ate the ones which were offered to him, and pronounced them delicious.

When he offered to pay, his money was waved away with desert courtesy. "Come, and bring your friends, to fall in love with my rugs", the man said, cocking his head to one side, like a wizened bird. "Don't you want to take one home, to your wife or your mother?" Rick shook his head, and wiped his sticky hands on a grimy towel.

"I have neither wife nor mother, but, if I had, I would surely give them one of your rugs", he said, climbing back into the Jeep. "By the way, where is a good place to sleep?"

"There are many places where a man may put his head, some better than others," the rug peddler said, not looking directly at him. "But you will find good food at the *Restaurant du Paradis*. Ask for my cousin, Amir."

The restaurant in Tozeur was situated just off the main street, by the post office. Men wearing dusty burnouses sat at the few outside tables, drinking coffee, and watching the tourists, who were in turn taking pictures of them. A camel herder, leading his arrogant looking pack animals, made his way down the center of the street. Rick parked the Jeep, and, despite the searing heat, strolled down the main street getting his bearings.

He ducked into the lobby of the first hotel he saw, finding it only a few degrees cooler, and only slightly less dusty. The proprietor seemed delighted to have a client, and ushered him to a room, which was a carbon copy of the one he had slept in the night before. He decided that all hotels outside Tunis must order their furniture from the same source. He threw his bag on the bed, washed his face in the brown, tepid water emerging from a broken faucet and sought the comfort of the street.

How to find a trace of Robbie? Among all of the towns which bordered the desert, Touzeur was the one which most tourists flocked to. It offered relatively easy access to tourist delights: camel herders, rolling sand dunes and yet was still not a long bus ride to civilization. It was also just across the border from Algeria. It was just the sort of place that would have attracted Robbie and his friends; just exotic enough to tempt them, yet seedy enough to fit their pocketbooks.

He pulled the sketch of Robbie, and his companions, from his pocket and looked at it again. It was a slight lead, but all he had, and the boys faces were clearly recognizable. The artist had caught the contrast between the American boys, and the Arabs, in an amusing, but clearly definable way. It was possible that someone might be able to identify them from this sketch. It was a slim chance, as he knew, but the only one he had, plus a photo of Robbie in his wallet.

He strolled down the street, mingling with the knots of tourists in pursuit of the cheapest rugs and dates. As he got closer to the market section of town, the crowd thickened, and so did the merchants selling their wares. He saw hash pipes being offered by one or two intrepid dealers. The pipes were strewn among a dozen less incriminating objects, but none the less boldly displayed.

Rick picked one up, feigning interest in the object, and turning it over carefully in his hands. The merchant, a thin young man wearing a boldly striped burnoose, watched him without comment. Rick balanced the oddly shaped, clay pipe in one hand, with the other, he presented the sketch of the four young men and a photograph of Robbie. The man looked at the photograph carefully for a second and then handed it back, shaking his head in disgust.

"It is not well to make images. The Koran forbids it," he spat.

"The Koran forbids many things that are done by men anyway." Rick said, placing the pipe carefully back on the mat, and walking away. He repeated this process with several other merchants, with similar results. Either no one had seen Robbie and his companions, or, as he suspected, they simply weren't talking. Anyhow, he had set the bait. Most of the market now knew that he was looking for some young men, who had either been buying or selling hashish. All he had to do now was to wait for someone to contact him to get a reward for his information.

The call wasn't long in coming. As he walked into his hotel, a smartly dressed, young, tourist policeman was waiting for him in the lobby. He spoke English, with an accent, which sounded middle American and invited Rick down to the police station, where his passport could be examined in private.

The Chief of Police welcomed him from behind a desk, lined with small, empty coffee cups. Rick recognized that each one of them indicated an interrogation finished, or a deal completed. He did not refuse, when offered one more cup. The Chief asked him what he was doing in Tozeur. After listening politely to his cover story, examining his passport, and then asked him why he was trying to purchase hashish when it was a crime in Tunisia, and punishable by prison. "And here, we throw away the key", he said, in French.

"And who told you that I was trying to purchase hash?", Rick asked, deciding that attack was the best defense under the circumstances.

"My under cover officers, who were trying to sell it to you", the Chief said, smilingly. "They were trained by a grant from your Department of State, under the AID program."

"Do I look like someone who would risk jail for a few ounces of hash?", Rick asked. "But I'm afraid that it has been used to entrap my son."

"Have you evidence of this?" The Chief asked, shifting his well fed girth behind his desk to reach for the sketches Rick extended to him.

"I have no evidence, except this sketch made by my friend Ben Hamid, in Sidi Bou Said."

The Police Chief nodded, seeming to recognize the name and style of the well-known Tunisian artist. "Which one is your son? And do you know the young men he is with?"

"If I did, and knew where they were, they would probably have their necks wrung by now", Rick answered, wryly. "Have you seen them?"

"If I had, they would probably be in prison by now", the Chief said, handing the sketches back to Rick. "The two Arab boys are Algerians, desert rats, who survive as they can, mostly by latching on to foreign tourists, and using them as a shield, to get small quantities of illegal drugs into Tunisia from Morocco through Algeria. After all, the Algerian border is only 25 kilometers away from here. The border is not well guarded, and a smuggler could be over and back from here in a matter of hours, especially if he used a four wheel drive vehicle and went across the desert, without the benefit of the road to Belima."

"And the other American boy?"

"I think in your country, you would call him a shill. The Algerians will use him, as long as is necessary to attract other American tourists, and then, when he is no longer of any use to them, they will get rid of him."

"And Robbie?"

"Your son is either working with them, or dead by now. These dealers leave no witnesses."

"But you said that they only bring in small quantities of drugs", Rick said, rubbing his forehead wearily.

"Yes, but multiply this group by many others working along the small border towns across the *Magreb*, and you have a network able to move many tons of drugs, and other illegal substances. No group necessarily knows about the other, and if you catch one and kill it, it is like slapping fleas."

"And there are always new, young tourists willing to take a chance and get free drugs?"

"Exactly, but like your son, they may find that it is the most expensive high they have ever had. They may end up paying with their lives."

"So what advice would you give me? How should I go about tracking him down?"

The policeman narrowed his eyes. "You may not like what you find. The two Algerians were through here several weeks ago, but, at that time, they were alone. We searched them, and finding nothing, put them on the road out of town. They may have gone toward D'Jerba. It's high tourist season there, and with so many plane loads coming and going, it's easy to get lost in the crowd."

"Could they have come back through here, later, with the two other boys, without you seeing them?", Rick asked.

"If they wished to avoid being seen, it would be easy enough for them to avoid my small police force, either going or coming from Algeria", he responded.

The Chief sipped his coffee noisily, and then got up, signifying that the interrogation was over, dismissing Rick with a wave of his hand, and the blessings of Allah on his journey.

Rick walked slowly back toward the hotel. The light was fading quickly, turning the desert around him into shimmering crimson, and then a dusty gold. He felt tired, and, for the first time, the hopelessness of what he was trying to do, swept over him. Looking for Robbie out here in the desert was beginning to look like an impossible task. A cloud of dust swept down the street, stirred by the tourist camels being led en masse to their watering place.

It finally occurred to him that he hadn't eaten, and that he was hungry. The *Restaurant du Paradis* was not hard to find, since it was one of two on the main street through town. Its window was framed by a set of ancient Christmas tree lights, that provided illumination for a copy of a fly specked menu. The restaurant was almost deserted, but at the insistence of his stomach, Rick entered.

The inside was dim and almost deserted. In the far corner, two men hunched over a table, covered with a checkered table cloth, which had seen better days. Rick chose a table near the window, where he could keep an eye on the comings and goings in the street. He was curious to see if anyone had followed him from the police station, but the street was almost as deserted as the *Restaurant du Paradis.*

A door swung open at the back of the restaurant and a heavy set man, wearing an oily head cloth, came forward to take Rick's order. He had eyes which were black and close together and he handed Rick a menu in English, greasy from the fingers of all the tourists who had come before him. "Are you Amir?" Rick asked, taking a chance.

The man looked startled, and pulled the menu back as though it might reveal something he didn't want Rick to know. "Have you been here before, Monsieur", he asked. "How do you know me?"

"Your cousin, the rug merchant, on the main road into town, told me to look for you, and for this restaurant. He said it was the best in Tozeur."

"And so it is", the man replied adjusting his headdress. "Here you will eat real Tunisian food, *brique* and cous cous and *tanjine*. Not food for the tourists. No hamburger, no hot dog, do we serve here."

"Well, then bring me whatever you recommend. I have a long journey ahead of me tomorrow to D'Jerba, and I will not have time for breakfast."

The man beamed and bowed. "I shall serve you myself. The very best Tunisian food. So you will remember, and you will tell your friends about the *Restaurant du Paradis* in Tozeur."

As Amir bustled away, brushing flies off the table with the sweep of his long sleeves. Rick gazed out at the street. Now it was so dark outside that he could see his own reflection in the window, and that of Amir, as he went through the room. Rick, in the reflection, saw him stop and whisper something to the two men near the kitchen door and as the door opened, he saw one of the men get up and follow Amir into the kitchen.

He waited quite some time before the kitchen door opened again, belching forth Amir, carrying a tray of crisply fried *brique*, which turned out to be philo dough, wrapped around ground meat, and a barely cooked egg. It tasted delicious. Eating it, however messily, Rick realized how hungry he had been. Amir stood beside him approvingly, watching him eat. With each course he served Rick seemed to rise in his estimation. Finally, after the lamb and cous cous, Rick gestured firmly that he had had enough.

Since he was now alone in the restaurant, with the departure of the second man from the table in the corner, he asked Amir to join him for coffee. The man looked startled, as though Rick had proposed something unthinkable. Rick gestured around the empty restaurant. "I don't think any of your other clients will mind. The place seems pretty empty, despite your excellent food."

The man looked at Rick with narrowed eyes. "It is not the season", he said cryptically, lowering himself into a chair. "The tourists who come now, only want to go on camel rides in the desert, not to eat real Tunisian food. It is a waste of time to cook for them." He looked Rick over curiously. "What are you looking for here in Tozeur?"

"Not rugs", Rick replied, sipping his coffee. He noticed, by the reflection in the window, that someone was now standing in the lighted kitchen door, as if listening to their conversation. He half turned, but whoever it was, retreated back into the shadows. "I thought that I might see something of the real desert."

"Then you should see the Desert Museum that belongs to my cousin. It is a tarantula ranch. He keeps them all in American cigarette boxes." Amir said, smiling through broken teeth and loading his coffee with more sugar.

"I don't have time, unfortunately. As I said, I leave for D'Jerba very early in the morning."

"To join all the other tourists?"

"No, to look for my son", Rick said quietly.

Amir looked at him thoughtfully. "To lose one's son is a difficult thing. A friend would help you find him."

"Unfortunately, I don't have many friends in this part of the world", Rick said, rising out of his chair, and dropping some bills on the table.

"Go to the Desert Museum in the morning, before you leave", Amir said, pocketing the bills. "Perhaps, you will find one there."

Rick slept fitfully that night. The room was close, despite the cold breeze off the desert. He kept half alert all night, as though expecting someone to join him. By first light, he was out of the hotel, leaving money for his room with a half-asleep boy, who was making the morning tea.

The cold desert air cleared his head. He drove back on the road he had come on, keeping an eye out for the Desert Museum. He didn't intend to stop, but some demon of curiosity compelled him to slow down, as he neared it. In looking for Robbie, he couldn't afford to leave any stone unturned, even a chancy one based upon Amir's last comment of the night before.

He pulled the Jeep over to the side of a stucco building bearing a sign, lettered in German and French with more imagination than accuracy. At this early hour, the place seemed deserted, with the exception of a few scrawny chickens scratching aimlessly for bugs.

However, at the back of the building, two women hovered over a large round clay pot, resting in the middle of wood fire. They looked at him curiously and, when he smiled at them, covered their faces and giggled. The bolder one uncovered the pot and pulled out a steaming round of freshly baked bread, which she offered to Rick. "*Hubbs tabuna,*" she said, smiling. "*Bayhe bayhe.*"

Rick warmed at the simple desert hospitality. The bread was so hot that he almost dropped it, causing the women to dissolve into another fit of giggles. But when he bit into it, it was thick and the taste was wheaty. It seemed to fill his mouth with a taste of home. The bread smelled of the firewood and of all good bakery things. He found himself hoping that Robbie had found some of this same kindness.

The back door swung open, and a stocky man came out, rubbing the sleep from his eyes. He looked Rick over carefully, and said something harshly to the women in Arabic. Then he smilingly extended his hand to Rick. In it he held a crumpled cigarette package. Rick shook his head silently.

The man grinned at him wickedly, showing gums that were almost bare of teeth and forced the opened package into Rick's hand. Rick dropped it quickly. As it hit the ground, a very angry tarantula emerged and scuttled rapidly along the ground toward Rick's foot. As Rick raised his foot to crush it, the man pushed him backwards, and with one swoop, deftly scooped the insect back into the box. Then he put his right hand to his heart and bowed. "Welcome to my tarantula farm, Sidi", he said, smiling. "What can I do for you?"

"Keep that blasted thing where it belongs, for one thing", Rick said, testily. "It's a little early in the morning for these kinds of games."

"What kind of games do you like, Sidi?", the man said, quietly. We have animals for all kinds of tastes here."

"I'm not a collector", Rick said, moving away from him. "I'm just a tourist on his way to D'Jerba. Amir told me to stop by."

The man's face took on a wily look. He studied Rick for a moment, and then invited him inside.

The small house was furnished sparsely. Recently occupied cots were on both sides of the room, with covers still crumpled. The "tarantula farmer", and museum owner, gestured at Rick to sit down on one of the cots, and, as if in apology, offered him a real cigarette. "Amir tells me that you are looking for your son. What is he doing alone in this country?"

"He is not alone. At least when he was last seen, he was with another American, and two Algerian boys, traveling across the *Magreb*. He was last seen in Sidi Bou Said, probably en route to the south, about three weeks ago. Do you know anything of boys like these?"

The man spat on the ground, and smiled showing his gums. Then he rubbed his thumb and forefinger together, in the international sign for money. "I might know, but you might not like to hear it."

Rick tossed him a bill. "Does a father not need to know about his only son, even if it is bad news? Tell me but only if it is the truth."

The man fingered the banknote, and sighed. Rick tossed him another. He folded it swiftly and put it into his pocket. "Two of the boys were here. They came to see the tarantulas, and to try to sell me some *keif keif*. They were bragging about an American boy, that they had sold to some bandits taking a truck across the border. They said he was fair skinned and had light hair." The man paused, and looked away.

Rick's stomach tightened. "What would bandits want with an American boy?"

The Arab looked sly. "What men do with boys is not known in your country?"

Rick suppressed an urge to strangle the museum owner, but dead, he could give no further information.

"Did they tell you where they had sold him?"

"Somewhere just across the border in the mountains in Algeria." He bragged. "It is easy for men to hide there. There are many caravans, and many of the Berbers are blonde. A light skinned boy would not attract too much attention." He narrowed his eyes. "But the boys who sold him were going to D'Jerba. That is where they do their business."

"And their business is?"

"What they do is against the Koran," the man said, simply. "Allah will punish them."

"Not if I get there first," Rick said, between clenched teeth.

It occurred to Rick, as he departed, that the Museum owner could be either misinformed, or lying, or both, just to supplement his obviously limited income from tarantula farming. It wouldn't be the first time in his experience that someone had told him what he thought Rick might want to hear, for a price.

Chapter Eight

Meanwhile, the other caravan was taking its time ambling toward D'Jerba. Janine had managed to follow von Grantz back to the fertilizer plant, but had seen even less than on her first visit. She had the distinct impression, that whatever was going on here, was not the full story. Now that Harrison was gone von Grantz seemed much too relaxed, as though he were treating the trip as a sightseeing journey.

Janine's contact at the Embassy had told her to stay close to von Grantz, and pick up any information she could. It was a task that she was finding increasingly unrewarding. The Germans spoke only to one another and then not often.

The Tunisian officer, Ahmed seemed to feel that keeping Janine under constant surveillance was his total duty. The group made painfully slow progress through the dusty small towns that lined the road to D'Jerba.

When they finally stopped for the night, Janine escaped to her room and a tepid shower. She again tried to make contact with her counterpart in D'Jerba on her cellular phone. Again, there was no answer. She had the uneasy feeling that she was riding into a trap. Perhaps that was what von Grantz was expecting when they got to Gafsa the next morning.

∗ ∗ ∗

Melanie had spent an exhausting two days, shopping in Paris, and trying to reach her father on the telephone. When both of these activities began to bore her at the same time, she booked a seat to Tunis on Air France. Then she sent a fax to her father, telling him of her flight plans and asking him to arrange for her to be met.

Dutifully, Duke Weston arranged with a well placed friend in the Department of State in Washington to send a fax to the American Ambassador in Tunis, asking that Melanie be met at the airplane and "extended the courtesies of the country in her search for her missing son."

At the same time, Weston called Jean Claude Bonet in Paris to tell him that finding his grandson was to be his top priority. Jean Claude headed up a foreign corporation, *Societe La Vente*, that couldn't be traced to Weston Enterprises, but, in actuality, belonged to Duke. This clandestine organization did all of those things that couldn't be done by an American entity, like trade in petroleum and chemicals with Libya, Iran, Cuba, and even Iraq, all countries with whom American corporations were prohibited from dealing with.

Jean Claude had been Duke Weston's trusted employee for years, knew Robbie and Melanie, and understood Duke's growing concern for the missing boy. Considering the resources of his organization, Jean Claude felt he could be helpful if it was in his own interest to do so. His own best interests being, as always, his primary concern.

The Ambassador received the news of Melanie's arrival less than enthusiastically. It seemed to him that he already had half of his staff chasing down information on this unfortunate young man, her son. The problem had done nothing but interfere with his tennis games for the last few days. However, given the amount of funds that Duke Weston had given in political contributions to the party in power, the request coming through the Department of State couldn't be ignored.

He called his wife, and asked her to put together a small dinner party, with politically correct people to meet the newcomer, thus causing his wife to have to cancel her hair appointment for the afternoon. This did not bode well for Melanie's arrival.

Melanie descended from the plane, and was met by a blast of hot, late afternoon air that might have come out of the wrong end of a vacuum cleaner. Her silk dress clung to her slight figure, and the hand, which she extended to the young diplomatic officer delegated to meet her, was limp with perspiration, and fatigue.

Upon hearing that a dinner had been scheduled in her honor for that evening, she declined, saying instead that she would rather go to bed early. The young officer was struck dumb. People didn't decline invitations to the Ambassador's residence. However, not knowing exactly how to communicate this to Melanie, he swallowed hard and directed the driver in Arabic to go directly to the hotel.

Once in the car, with air conditioning turned on, Melanie gained some interest in her surroundings. She also noticed that the officer, despite his youth, was very good looking in a clean cut sort of way and impeccably dressed. She invited him to join her at the hotel for a swim, an invitation he politely refused, saying that he was expected early at the Ambassador's party.

"Why, than I'll come too. It might be fun." Melanie said with one of those lightning changes of mood for which she was famous, thereby eliminating the chance of a diplomatic incident the night of her arrival.

*　　　*　　　*

Rick drove doggedly through the desert toward D'Jerba. Nothing he had learned about Robbie had reassured him at all. He had thought briefly about going across the border into Algeria, but with the increasing political unrest in that country, that would have been playing a wild card, and probably unproductive. The more he thought about it, the more skeptical he was of the Tarantula farmer's information.

He was without backup. It would be next to impossible to track the Algerians down if they had gone any further than the border town. He was going to have to find a another way to trace Robbie. Perhaps, when he got to D'Jerba, Janine would have some news and her man in D'Jerba could provide backup for a mission into war torn Algeria.

Nothing he had learned so far had been in the least reassuring. But it all seemed to fit together in some strange way that he couldn't yet fathom. The chemical plants, the drugs going easily back and forth across a border that was supposed to be secure against them, the kidnapping, and the alleged Algerian bandits reported to him by the Museum owner. The penalty for illegal drugs in Tunisia was high, that was well known, but evidently not a deterrent in this case.

All of this to serve some purpose. But what was it? And how did Robbie and his friends fit into this picture? If they were just pawns in some greater struggle, why hadn't they been eliminated without a trace? That was easy enough to do in a wasteland like this. Why was Robbie being held and by whom and where? What did his captors hope to obtain? He had to believe that Robbie was still alive, somewhere. Otherwise, all of this made no sense at all. Like the rest of his life at this moment.

As he drove down the long lonely road, he passed an occasional Land Rover bound in the opposite direction. His rudimentary map indicated that the next town of any size was Kebili, and beyond that, Matmata and the home of the Troglodites, or cave dwellers. It was a barren wasteland where tourists came infrequently. It might possibly be a place where a young American boy could be detained, without attracting much attention.

He looked at the sky and then noticed in the rear view mirror, a curious cloud of dust on the road behind him. It seemed to stay just out of the range of his vision, but it was moving too fast to be a herd of animals and too slowly to be a vehicle trying to pass him.

He kept it in view for a half hour or so, while it continued to follow him and then decided to take the initiative to stop and see if the vehicle passed him. The cloud of dust came closer, and finally an old Harley Davidson motorcycle, ridden by a thin young man, covered with dust, emerged from it, and stopped. Off of it got a young, dark skinned man, wearing jeans, a cut off tee shirt and mirrored sunglasses. He took off the glasses, polished , and replaced them, while waiting for Rick to speak.

"Good looking wheels", Rick said casually, in French, as the young man looked at him arrogantly over the top of his designer sunglasses. "I didn't know that they imported those into Tunisia."

"I've got connections" the Arab muttered, kicking at the ground at his feet. The dust rose into the air like fine talcum powder, settling back down over them like a kind of benediction. "What are you doing on this road anyhow? It's not a safe place for tourists."

"If I'd wanted to be safe, I guess I'd have stayed at home", Rick answered, rocking back on his heels. There was something odd about the young man, not menacing exactly, just odd.

"Well, it's a good idea to stay out of lonely places, man, you never know who you might meet".

As the young man moved toward him, Rick noticed how dilated his pupils were. His dark eyes seemed to be focused on something beyond them both. Rick had seen drugged out killers before in his other life as an intelligence officer, but this one looked as though his brains were fried. Rick sidestepped, as the man lurched forward, and with a skill, born of long practice, twisted his arm behind his back, and forced him to his knees.

The man began to babble incoherently, twisting and squirming to get out of Rick's grasp. He was sweating profusely, yet his skin felt cold to Rick's hands, as though he were already dead.

Rick pulled the Arab to his feet, and after patting him down for a weapon, took away the long, evil looking knife that seemed his only means of defense. "Who sent you?", he asked, shaking the young man like a dead rabbit. "Who told you to follow me?"

The man whined, and pulled away, then began shaking as though he had been hit in the spine by a missile. He let out a gasp, and foam began to come out of his mouth. Rick loosened his hold, the man dropped to the ground, and was still.

Moving carefully in case of a trap, Rick dropped to his knees in the dust, and felt the Arab's neck and his pulse. They were quiet. He rolled the young man over on his back. His eyes were wide open, staring at something that he could no longer see. He carried no identification, and had nothing in his pockets but a modest roll of dinars in large denominations. The Harley was also without identification. Rick pushed it to the side of the road, and rolled the young man's body beside it. He could report it to the police later.

Rick climbed back into the Jeep, and shifted it into gear. There was no one else to be seen on the road or on the horizon. Rick felt as though he was lost on the moon.

Why did someone keep sending these amateurs against him? Or was he just getting paranoid in this god forsaken country. Maybe this was just some drugged out kid that thought he would be an easy mark. He didn't look much older than Robbie, though his face had some early lines of dissipation. There was no one in sight, and nothing apparent, that could have killed him. He must have bought it on some kind of drug overdose. But why here? And why with him?

Rick glanced at his watch. He'd better step on it if he wanted to reach Matmata, and the Troglodite villages before dark. Perhaps there would be a prefect there to whom he could report the incident. Maybe, he should leave that to the next traveler. He had had a bad moment, leaving the boy's body there next to the Harley. He hoped that, whoever came along next, would think that it was just a motorcycle accident and report it. He wanted less and less to get involved with anyone or anything here. He just wanted to find Robbie, get out of the country and get back to the life he had made for himself, such as it was.

*   *   *

Janine stretched luxuriously, feeling her body rubbing against the rough sheets and wiggling her toes to free them from the scratchy blankets. Today was the day that von Grantz would make his move. She felt it in her bones, and like a fighter ready for action, she was ready for this encounter. She felt better with her enemy out in the open, and her instinct told her that Gafsa was going to be part of the answer to the puzzle.

The Tunisians had been working on building a factory there for several years. Because of a series of mishaps reported through the grapevine, but never discussed openly, it still hadn't been put into operation. Word had it that some of the promised equipment had not yet arrived from the German firm that was overseeing the construction. Janine's sources told her that it might be a cover for an entirely different kind of operation.

Shipments of various chemicals, even including plutonium, had been diverted from other clients, and were slowly finding their way into this part of the world. With the border between Tunisia, Algeria and Libya, essentially unguarded in most places, this was not difficult to achieve. Five militant Islamic groups were now struggling for power in Algeria, leaving the government there little time or resources to patrol the borders. The conflict was supposed to be as bad as it was during the Algerian civil war, but the newspapers had, on the whole, ignored it. There were more easily understood conflicts going on in the world at the moment.

Janine took her automatic out of her briefcase, and fastened it to the back of her belt. A glance in the mirror at the back of her jacket assured her that it could not be seen. She pulled her honey colored hair back into a severe bun, and fastened it tightly with a rubber band. The combination of the severe hair do, and the weight of the pistol at the small of her back made her feel confident and ready for anything von Grantz had to offer. She would have felt even more confident, if she were sure which side the Tunisian officer would be on if trouble started.

Before leaving the room, she tried once more, unsuccessfully, to phone the agent in D'Jerba. The unanswered ringing of the telephone told her that, as usual, she was on her own.

From a childhood in what was then East Germany she had learned early to be alone, and what it took to survive. As the illegitimate child of an American GI father, and a German mother, she had belonged no place, and to no one. Working for the Agency was the first legitimacy she had found and she was determined not to lose it. She had gained her place in the ranks by a combination of toughness and the calculated use of her feminine wiles, which had left other agents in her dust and had gained her few friends, among her peers.

Harrison was a retread, and evidently not a very good one at that, from what she had seen so far. She felt better off without him. She was used to covering her own backside. This was the time when she could finally prove that she could do it on her own. Women were just beginning to make some real progress in the Agency. She wanted one of the good jobs in Washington when she left Tunisia; she had already worked long and hard for it. She would complete this assignment with or without Harrison and if it was without him, that was all right.

She greeted Grantz in her impeccable German, receiving another astonished glance from him for her trouble.

Ahmed watched her with an amused smile, which told her that he enjoyed watching the German squirm. It was going to be a hot ride this morning to Gafsa, and any diversion at all was welcome. Even watching this American woman annoy the German scientists was amusing. He expected to get her into bed before the tour was over, and until then he enjoyed observing her.

She seemed even more sure of herself now that the other American was gone. Or perhaps, she was just a good actress. At any rate, he liked the way she carried herself, straight and tall, as though she had a rifle up her back.

The ride to the south was uninspiring. They passed a few camel drivers, and a number of tourists in their rented cars, driving as though their lives depended on getting to the next oasis before dark. Janine knew the feeling. She was already gritty and sweaty from sitting in the car, and the sun wasn't yet up to its full height.

They reached Gafsa mid-morning, and without stopping even for a cold drink, made their way to the half constructed fertilizer factory on the outskirts of town. It looked as though a dozen different attempts had been made to finish it, and then abandoned. The cement was of different colors and consistencies, and cavernous rooms stretched out in several directions on the sun baked earth. Some were roofed and covered, and some were still open to the elements. A construction trailer seemed to serve as a kind of office. It was toward this that the dusty group directed its steps.

A small Tunisian in a baggy uniform greeted them at the door. He looked at them suspiciously until Ahmed addressed him in Arabic. Then his features softened somewhat, and he invited them into his office. The room seemed to contain all of his worldly belongings, most of them on the floor. Welcoming them with a gesture, he invited them to sit and take tea. Von Grantz cast a stern look toward the Tunisian officer and shook his head firmly. Clearly he had reached his tolerance for Arab hospitality.

With some prodding, the local director, Brahim, agreed to show them around the site, which was deserted except for a few stray chickens, pecking disconsolately in the dust. He waved his arms expansively, gesturing to the right and left and talking rapidly in Arabic, indicating with his arms the grandeur of the government's plans for this remote location.

Janine found herself wondering why the project had been delayed so long, and what had happened to all the American funds contributed to its construction so far. In her official position as Assistant Commercial Attaché, she had seen letters from AID, directing substantial amounts to this factory. Where had all the money gone, and what was this exceptionally large site really intended for?

It looked very unlike the other fertilizer factory they had seen. The concrete walls in some places were ten feet thick. Surely that was a lot of security for a plant using the relatively benign chemicals needed to make fertilizer or insecticides. Perhaps some of the smuggled plutonium coming into the country had been intended originally for this site.

Von Grantz, and his assistant, were carefully inspecting the unfinished factory on foot. They measured the walls, and the distances between them and then went back and measured again. It was late afternoon when they finished. Janine, sitting in the shadow of a wall, fanned herself with her hat. She saw no need of following von Grantz around, let the Tunisian do that. Whatever there was to see here, could be clearly seen in an hour. Von Grantz was either using delaying tactics, or he knew something that she didn't about the intended use of the buildings.

She glanced idly around the site. Something certainly was not right about this construction, something that she was missing. For the moment, she regretted that Harrison wasn't with them. He did have a greater expertise than she did in chemical factories and what to expect from them.

Janine glanced at her watch. It was getting late, and if they didn't start soon, they would arrive in D'Jerba after dark, not something that she was looking forward to. It would also give her less time to contact her agent.

Suddenly, she heard voices arguing in Arabic. They seemed to be coming closer, and getting angrier. She stood up, and leaned into the shadow of a wall. Two men came toward her, arguing so vehemently that they seemed unaware of her presence, until they were almost on top of her. Then they leapt at her, one covering her mouth with his hands, while the other threw an evil smelling blanket around her, pinning her arms to her sides, and lifting her off the ground, doubled over like a sack of grain.

Janine tried to scream, and kicking viciously against the assailants, struggled unsuccessfully to reach for her gun. Her arms were pinned to her sides by the heavy rug. The smell made her feel as though she were drowning in camel urine. Her writhing felt as though she were scratching all the skin off her face. She decided to stop moving and play dead, hoping to catch her captors off guard.

They were talking to one another now, in urgent voices, as they dragged her along the bumpy ground. Where were Ahmed and the others? Were they too busy inspecting the site to notice that she had disappeared, or was this von Grantz's plan, to have her simply vanish from Gafsa, as women had vanished many times before her in the Arab world.

Her trick of becoming a dead weight seemed to be working somewhat. Her captors were moving more slowly, and their breathing was becoming labored as their arguing increased. Janine struggled not to black out, as she tried to suck in air through the thick camel hair rug. All the tricks she had learned in self defense ran through her mind, but most of them used a part of her anatomy, which was at the moment inoperable.

Using all her strength, she was able to execute a quick seal-like maneuver, which threw one of her captors off balance. As he turned to kick the blanket, he lost his balance and dropped her on the ground instead, knocking the breath out of her and filling her teeth with camel hair.

She heard a shout from the distance, and then a gun shot. A foot kicked at her wildly again, and was gone. She lay prone for a minute, in the evil smelling blanket, regaining her breath. Then she felt her cocoon being slowly unwound. The Tunisian army had come to the rescue in the form of Ahmed. His worried face looked down at her. She struggled to her feet, with all the dignity she could muster under the circumstances. Her hair was in her face, her were clothes covered with dirt and camel hair from the rug was stuck to her skin. She smelled strongly of camel piss. "Thanks for the help" she muttered.

"Are you all right?" the Tunisian officer asked grimly.

"Except for the perfume of camel urine", Janine answered wryly. "And to answer your question, I've never seen them before."

Von Grantz and his assistant ran up with Brahim chattering wildly in Arabic behind them. When Ahmed questioned the two about the incident, they said that they had been too engrossed in scientific measurements to see what had happened. Brahim, on the other hand, was almost prostrate trying to explain. Clearly he was worried that he would be held responsible. He swore to Allah that he knew nothing about the men or their intentions.

Janine, seeing the anger on Ahmed's face tried to make light of the incident. Dusting herself off, she suggested that they go somewhere where she could wash up and then they could continue onto D'Jerba. "We can talk in the car", she assured Ahmed, who was intent on finding and punishing the guilty. Her useless pistol was poking her in the back, and she longed to get somewhere private to rearrange it. But the tall Arab wouldn't let her out of his sight. He now seemed to consider her his own private booty.

As they jounced along toward D'Jerba, Janine began to try to put the day's incidents into some kind of pattern. At the moment, it eluded her. Von Grantz and his assistant were in such a good mood, that it seemed clear they had found something of value in the cement and iron pile they had spent the afternoon inspecting. To Janine, it looked like a colossal waste of money, more than justifying any Senate committee's doubts about the efficacy of the US AID program.

But whatever Grantz had found had cheered him up immensely. Perhaps that was what her "abduction" had been about. Maybe it had just been a ploy to get her out the way for a while, not to put her totally out of commission. That might have raised too many questions. It was clear that whoever had sent Grantz, was trying to keep a low profile and limit information, while getting the job done.

*   *   *

Duke Weston looked at the report coming in by especially secured fax. What he saw didn't please him. He was a man who liked to be in control and to play power games. It bothered him when his games backfired or didn't pay off. It was like losing at poker, and Duke didn't like to lose. He had kept his company strong, with all the commodities he needed to play international poker.

Weston Enterprises, and its subsidiaries, clandestine or overt, in addition to oil leases in many countries, controlled enough of the basic chemicals in the United States, used in fertilizer, insecticides and pesticides, to supply most of the needs of Europe and the Middle East. What the end use of the chemicals was, was not his problem. and where he and his customers got their oil wasn't either.

The trouble was that now it was getting harder and harder to bet on the winner, the players changed so fast. These Muslims, particularly the religious ones, were tricky customers. You never really knew which side they were on. They killed as easily as they breathed, all in the name of Allah, and their appetite for arms, of one kind or another, was voracious. Their ability to pay, up until now, at least, was equal to their appetite.

But now with the PLO apparently playing ball with the Israelis, and various terrorist groups sprouting up all over the world, the game was changing. It was getting more desperate and nastier all the time, and his clients' ability to pay was no longer certain.

And right smack in the middle of it all was Robbie. It seemed that his captors had not yet connected him to Weston Enterprises. If no one had made the connection, he might already be dead, since it was a little late in the game for a ransom note.

Damn Harrison! What was the use of having an ex-CIA agent for an ex-son in law, if he couldn't find his own son in an area with which he was familiar? Rick had been in Tunisia four days already, and had managed to find out nothing. At the moment, though, Duke's operatives couldn't find him either. Robbie just seemed to have disappeared, without a visible trace, as far as the American Embassy, Rick and Weston Enterprises could determine.

Chapter Nine

The rolling hills of southern Tunisia were barren and brown. Only a few scattered herds of sheep could survive there, and the old shepherd who watched them took his living from the land just as they did. The shepherd had lived in these hills all his life, served Allah faithfully, prayed to Mecca and tried to live in peace with his fellow man, when he saw one, which was rarely.

He belonged to a time when a man was grateful and accepted where he was and what he had as the will of Allah. He ate his food, watched his sheep, said his prayers and lived and died as his fathers had before him.

But now things were beginning to change. There were young men with guns in the desert. They came and went as swiftly as the night. They boasted of how many men they had killed, Frenchmen especially. They said that they were doing it in the name of Allah, to purify Islam. The old man, Mabrouk, had lived all his life thinking that Islam was pure.

He breathed deeply and covered his eyes from the late afternoon sun with his gelaba. Lately, there had been trucks crossing the desert. They crossed at night on trails marked by half-buried oil drums. The trucks came from the west and they came in the dark, but the old man could hear them, with his ears so attuned to the sound of the night. He knew when something, other than his sheep, was moving in the night.

One of the young men who drove the trucks had tried to talk with him, to buy a sheep to kill. But the old man told them that his sheep were not for sacrifice. The young man had taken it anyhow, swearing a curse and throwing money on the ground. Nothing good would come of this, nothing at all. The meaning of Islam was to endure, but these young men were beyond endurance.

The world was changing. He hoped that he would die before it changed too much. If these young men were what the future would be like, he would take his sheep deeper into the hills and when the time came, he would die. He would fold his gelaba around himself, point his head toward Mecca and go to join his fathers.

∗ ∗ ∗

The two young men drove deeper into the desert. The sheep, that they had taken from the old shepherd, was bleating in the back of the truck, like someone pleading for his life. The older of the two glanced over his shoulder into the darkening desert. He cradled a rifle on his knees and narrowed his eyes against the setting sun.

The Frenchwoman had been hard to kill. She had bleated like this sheep at the last. She was an intruder in his country. He had to purify it, to purge Islam of all infidels. Then the land would be pure again, for Allah.

The sheep bleated again. He nodded to his companion, who stopped the truck just long enough to slit its throat and stop its bleating. They would skin and roast it when they got to the safe place.

He licked his lips and wondered if the fair haired boy was still there. The one their leader called the blonde infidel. Or had he already been given to someone else for his pleasure, before he was killed. The leader was not always fair in these matters. He did not always reward everyone equally. But surely killing twelve Frenchmen and one of their women should be worth some kind of reward.

He licked his lips again and waited. If his leader did not reward him, then Allah would. He would kill the blonde infidel.

∗ ∗ ∗

Robbie opened his eyes, and looked around the room. He was alone. Usually when he woke up, someone was watching him. He was weak from not moving, and his head swam, when he tried to sit up. He didn't know where he was or what had happened to him. He remembered the sound of men's voices, and the smell of urine. Looking down, he realized that it was his own. The bed was filthy, and some of the filth was his.

He tried to stand up, but the tether on his legs was too short, and besides, his head hurt too much. There was water in a jug beside the bed. He took some of it to drink, and tried to wash his face with the rest. It didn't do much good, but the effort made him feel better. If he could just get away from the stench of this room. The stench that he had created from the looks of it.

He wondered if he should call out. He seemed to be in some kind of cave. There was light coming from the entrance, which was covered with a kind of matted cloth. He strained his ears, but could hear nothing. Maybe they had gone off and left him alone. That thought was almost as frightening as what they had done to him.

Who were they and what did they want? He lay down again to keep his head from hurting so much, and fought against the sleep that was threatening to engulf him again.

He began to recite a prayer that his mother had taught him. "Now I Lay me down to sleep", and felt the slow tears burning the corner of his eyes, and sliding down his face. He tried to remember his mother's perfume to blank out the stench of his own body. Her perfume was soft and sweet, like jasmine. If only he could smell it again. Touch her soft hands. Tell her that he loved her, and that he was sorry, so sorry for what he had done.

Outside, the men had gathered to welcome their comrades back from the "hunt". The sheep was quickly skinned and cleaned, and a small fire begun for roasting. The leader appeared from his tent, and took the best share of the meat for himself. Then he sent someone to the cave to look in on Robbie.

"The boy is awake, but he has soiled himself", the man reported.

"Then wash him, and give him clean clothing", the leader ordered. "Tomorrow is the beginning of the feast of Ramadan. Even infidels must be clean," he smiled showing broken front teeth. "When the boy is clean, bring him to me. We will see why those camel drivers treated him so carefully."

Robbie blinked, and tried not to cry out, as he was dragged into the late afternoon sunlight and doused with dirty water that smelled of camel dung. The men laughed, and made remarks as they ripped his dirty and stained clothes off his body, and rubbed him roughly with sand. The gelaba they threw at him to put on was rough gray cotton and was much too long for his thin frame but at least it smelled clean. Then they twisted his arms behind his back with a leather thong, blindfolded him and pushed him toward the center of the camp.

Robbie stumbled and almost fell, but the pressure of a rifle in his back kept him moving. His legs trembled, and ached from inaction and he felt like throwing up. But he kept moving. Something told him that showing any signs of weakness would be his death. He bit his lip so hard that he could taste his own blood.

He felt the warmth of a fire against his legs, and someone pushed him roughly to his knees, bruising them against the rough sand and stones. He heard voices speaking in Arabic and then a man's voice, deeper than the others, seemed to be addressing him in broken English.

"So my little American, Allah has sent you to us as a hostage against the money the camel drivers owe us. Do you think that they will come and buy you back? Or will they leave you here with us to do with you as we like. We might even cut your throat tomorrow, instead of the sheep they promised us. Do you think that Allah would accept you instead of a sheep as a sacrifice for our celebration of Ramadan? I'm sure that my men would prefer the sheep." He laughed evilly.

Robbie shivered and a long shudder passed through his whole body, as though a giant hand were shaking him. He tried to speak, but no words came. He was using all his strength to keep from crying. Someone pulled the blindfold from his eyes and shoved him forward so that his head touched the ground.

The men laughed. "The little American is bowing toward Mecca. He is a true Arab", the man with the deep voice roared, laughing as he said it. "Let us see which other of our customs he will adopt. Perhaps, we can teach him to dance like a woman, and entertain us. There are no women here. We must make the best of what we have."

And with that the games began, and lasted until the fire was burned to embers and Robbie lay sobbing beside it, wanting only to die.

* * *

Rick woke from a dream that was so intense that his muscles were tight and his hands clenched in fists. The dream was of Robbie. He was in terrible trouble and calling out for help. He was screaming and sobbing for someone to save him. In his dream, Rick stood by helpless, and watched the boy being tortured. Robbie was somewhere in a barren open place that could have been anywhere in the desert. Rick awoke, knowing that the dream was somehow real and that he didn't have much time left to save his son.

Because of internal conflict that was daily getting worse in Algeria, the hinterlands were virtually unpoliced. People wanting to evade notice, or to get away with smuggling drugs or anything else, would have a pretty clear time of it, as far as the authorities were concerned. There were at least five extremist groups struggling for power. Robbie might be in the clutches of any one of them.

Tunisia was generally a well policed democracy, in contrast with Algeria, but in the south and in the desert or the mountains, government was among the tribes. Rick was more and more convinced that his answers lay somewhere in that region and that now was the time to find him before it was too late.

One thing he had to do was to get a message to headquarters, somehow. He had been out of contact for too long. He had the emergency number in Tunis, if he could find a telephone that worked. His cellular was out of range.

He was sleeping in a Troglodite village, with one of the underground homes turned into a picturesque bed and breakfast by two hospitable Frenchmen. He had not seen a telephone, but that didn't prove that one didn't exist, hidden inside an earthenware pot somewhere. There was none in his room, but as he climbed onto the terrace in the early morning sun, he was greeted by one of his hosts in tight levis and a red, sleeveless undershirt, which showed off his biceps.

"*Mais oui*, Monsieur", he said, rolling his eyes. "We have a telephone and even a fax machine. Do follow me into the office. This is where the cast stayed, when they shot Star Wars, many years ago."

Rick followed him, observing the languid roll of his hips, as he walked. Pickings must be poor in this part of the country, if he was coming on to a client. But perhaps that was why some men came to this out of the way place. He thought again of Robbie, with a stab of pain. He would kill the man who touched him that way; strangle him with his bare hands if necessary.

He sent a terse fax to his office, one to Sam Shepherd at the Embassy in Paris and phoned the number Janine had given him in Tunis. As expected, that number was an answering machine. He left a coded message about his change of plans.

Rick asked his disappointed host for a map and some food and filled his extra jerry cans with water. Then he climbed into his Jeep and was on his way before the sun was fully up over the horizon. Instead of going toward D'Jerba, though, he headed back toward Tozeur and the Algerian border. He would have to leave Janine on her own. She was a tough lady and would survive. Everything that he had heard so far about Robbie pointed to the region somewhere south between Tozeur and the Algerian border, or across it into no-man's land.

He knew that this was a wild shot, but he had to take it. Something about the dream stayed with him, just out of reach. It was almost as though he could see the place where Robbie was being held prisoner. If he could get across the Algerian border unobserved, following the route of the camel caravans, he might have a chance. Otherwise, it might already be too late.

*   *   *

Sam sat in his office, fingering a copy of a fax from Duke Weston. The old boy was really getting upset. It must anger him to find something that he couldn't fix, or change with a bribe, or a large check written to the right political campaign.

It was too bad that this had to happen over Robbie. He fervently hoped that the kid was all right. The message Harrison had left worried him. It wasn't like him to desert a mission and go off on his own on a wild goose chase. He must really be worried about his son, which was easily understandable, or else he was on to something big. Sam preferred to think the latter. He couldn't imagine Harrison bailing out in the middle of a mission and he must know that, in Algeria, he was out of range of anything but the most minimal help. The sides in that conflict were changing so fast that it was impossible to know your friends from your enemies, and it was certain that an American operative on his own would find that he had plenty of the latter.

To all intents and purposes Harrison was behaving like a wild card and, in the chain of command, it would be Sam who would be held responsible for choosing him and retrofitting him for duty. He pressed a button on his desk and looked at a map of the Sahara that was uncovered. He had been tracking Harrison's progress as the meager reports came in.

It now looked as though he was headed out across some desolate country that was usually available only to camel drivers in the good season. The only trump card was that it was country that was normally of no interest to anyone. If Harrison didn't get himself killed by bandits or mercenaries, he might have a chance of surviving out there. The big question was why was he taking the chance. It must be Robbie.

*   *   *

As Rick headed out of the small village, he wondered just how to approach crossing the border after reaching Tozeur. His hosts had assured him that he would not be far from the Algerian border when he reached Tozeur, but why he would want to go there they couldn't imagine. He explained that he was a photo journalist after some unusual shots of the nomad population.

"You'll be lucky if you find only camels," his host had said wrinkling his nose. Those mountains are filled with people who don't want to be found or photographed. Why don't you just stay here, and photograph the Troglodite villages. After all, as we told you before, this is where Lucas shot the first Star Wars. Your magazine would love it."

Rick had nodded noncommittally, as he packed his gear into the Jeep. He promised to return in three days, or if he didn't return, he left instructions to call the Embassy in Tunis.

He had a sneaking feeling that the Ambassador might be just a little bit happy to get rid of him. So far he hadn't turned up much that was of any use. And what he knew, the Tunisians were sure to have already learned.

Where did Janine fit into all of this? She was certainly an operative, but just which side was she on?

He had a fleeting moment of regret for having left her on her own with the German team, and the Tunisian officer. But then he grinned, as the road got rougher and bumpier. He had a feeling that this was one lady who always landed on her feet. She had a core of steel inside that seductive body.

*   *   *

Janine, at that moment, was trying to locate her operative in D'Jerba. The group was on the less inhabited side of the island. They had agreed mutually to stay out of the tourist district and had settled into a small hotel made like a copy of one of the traditional houses. It was flat roofed and surrounded by a courtyard. In front of it lay an empty sandy beach with inviting turquoise blue water licking the shore.

Janine longed to put on her suit and go for a swim. She decided to do just that as soon as her traveling companions were out of the way. She also needed to call the Embassy on the "clean" line and see if anyone there knew what had happened to their man in D'Jerba.

The "clean" line rang and rang, but there was no answer, not even a machine. She tried the Embassy number she had given Rick, got his message, and left a message for the Ambassador as to where she could be reached.

Then she decided to go for a swim anyhow. It didn't look as though anyone else was around. The water was warm and closed around her, like the arms of a lover. She turned over on her back and swam out away, keeping an eye on the shore. The waves were gentle ripples and pulled her playfully after them, farther and farther from the beach.

She saw von Grantz come out of his room and look out to sea. He was joined by his pudgy aide, who shaded his eyes searching the coastline. Janine knew that she was probably too far out to be recognized. But what were they looking for, if not her? Or what were they expecting?

She looked over her shoulder and saw only a few small fishing boats positioned off shore. The boats seemed almost deserted, except for a lone fisherman, or two, sitting listlessly in them, as though waiting for the fish to jump into the boat.

Janine turned and began to swim parallel to the shoreline. There was almost no current pulling against her now and she was able to put herself quickly out of von Grantz's line of sight, in case he was looking for her. She was at the far left of the hotel beach, parallel with a dusty line of palm trees with a pile of pots at their base, guarded by what looked like an elderly woman.

Von Grantz was now gesticulating, in an effort to catch someone's attention off shore. But still only the fishermen were evident and they seemed not to be interested in the German's gyrations.

As Janine began to paddle toward shore, one of the fishing boats pulled away from the others and started in her direction. As the boat came closer, she could see that the man, at the helm of the small outboard, didn't look like a Tunisian. He had the heavier features and the lighter skin of a European, even though he was wearing a traditional gelaba.

He seemed not to have caught sight of her, or if he had, he was more interested in getting closer to the beach and von Grantz and his aide, while at the same time, trying not to draw attention to himself.

Janine started to tread water, watching him closely. Now, von Grantz and his aide, had also caught sight of the boat and they loitered on the beach, making a show of picking up shells and examining them closely. Janine grinned. The image of the stern German as a shell collector was more than she could stand. His sidekick Hanz looked like a disheveled German school boy on summer vacation.

She swam under water for a few yards, moving out of range of the boat. She was beginning to feel waterlogged and a little chilly, even though the water was warm. She kicked slowly towards the shore, still keeping an eye on von Grantz and the fishing boat.

The boat pulled almost onto the beach and von Grantz, and his partner, waded out to it. Then the fisherman pulled them aboard. They managed the maneuver awkwardly, like men unused to physical exertion. The fisherman handed them each a package which contained plastic pullover jackets. When they had donned these, he gunned the motor, and von Grantz and his companion were soon out of sight.

"I wonder what that was all about," Janine mused, as she paddled towards shore. They hadn't taken any pains to hide what they were doing. Meeting an operative in broad daylight in the middle of the bay wasn't exactly classic espionage technique. But they certainly didn't look as though they were going fishing. And why the plastic jackets? It wasn't going to rain, and the boat wasn't kicking up enough spray to get them wet.

They might be off to inspect another hidden site. Perhaps there was something hidden in the caves along the island's north shore. If special materials were coming into D'Jerba that no one was to know about, then there must be some safe place to store them on the island before they were shipped inland.

Again, she wished briefly for Harrison's expertise, and was genuinely sorry that she hadn't been more help in locating his son. The current thinking at the Embassy was that the boy was probably already dead. If he had been mixed up with drug smugglers, the chances of his still being alive were pretty slim. Kids of his age were used, if they were stupid enough to get involved, and then tossed aside like so much garbage. But it had been hard to tell a father that about his son. Better to let him find the evidence himself and draw his own conclusions.

She pulled herself ashore, feeling waterlogged, and jog trotted back to her hotel room. Ahmed was just emerging from his room freshly showered and holding a small cup of black Arab coffee He saluted her with it and asked her to join him. She accepted, the coffee smelled wonderful, and she was curious to know if Ahmed had seen von Grantz and company leave, and if he had any idea of where they were going.

Ahmed glanced admiringly at her slender figure in the clinging wet suit. Janine quickly wrapped her towel firmly under her arms, cutting off his view, but not his slightly lascivious look.

"Your coffee smells great. Thanks for the offer," she said, shivering slightly.

"To fulfill your desire, is my pleasure", he said in Arabic and poured some of the inky coffee into the cup from a small thermos he had on the table beside him. "You see, I always come prepared to serve a woman whatever she wants", he said, glancing again at Janine's eyes, lips and body, as he handed her the cup.

She smiled graciously, ignoring the invitation to engage in sexual banter. He was taller and stronger than she and could probably overpower her, if he were so inclined. At any rate, she didn't want to tempt him, knowing the proclivities of Tunisian males.

She sat down on the sand cross legged and hugged the coffee cup to her as if she were freezing, depending upon the Tunisian's native courtesy to turn the conversation elsewhere.

"Von Grantz and his aide have disappeared," she said controlling a shiver. "Do you have any idea where they have gone?"

"No, but they were finally in an unholy hurry to get to D'Jerba", he said, watching her with his liquid, dark eyes half closed. "May we surmise that they have something on their minds, besides the inspection of our fertilizer plants?"

He took the cup from her and refilled it. The hot sweet liquid was like a life force flowing through her.

"I think, Miss Janine, that it is time that we, as you say in America, put our cards on the table. We are both after the same thing, though perhaps we are approaching it from different angles. With your friend Harrison off on a wild goose chase and the two Germans gone from the hotel, it looks as though what is left, for the moment, is just the two of us. I suggest that we play on the same team. Otherwise we may end up getting each other killed and perhaps for the wrong reason."

Janine shifted her position in the sand, handing him back the cup. This was the longest speech that she had ever heard the officer make. She had assumed that he was a low level *fonctionaire* sent along to keep an eye on the situation and to report back to Tunis for instructions, when necessary.

His speech just now indicated that he knew more about the mission than she had supposed. Could she really trust him? She decided to hedge her bets.

"I would just like to know what these two Germans are really up to", she said, shaking the wet hair out of her face. "We've come a long way just to have them disappear in broad daylight."

"But perhaps you and I are better off with them gone", he said, moving closer to her." We can—how do you say it in English?—cement relationships between our two countries?"

Janine rolled over and up, out of his grasp, pretending not to understand the sexual invitation in his voice.

"I think that my next move is to get dried off for dinner. That coffee just made me hungrier. But thanks anyhow", she said, deliberately misunderstanding his tone.

"When Allah wills", he answered, watching her with something like amusement, and toying with the edge of her towel. "If von Grantz does not return, then perhaps shall have dinner alone. Just the two of us."

*   *   *

Von Grantz and his compatriot were sitting low in the fisherman's small boat, which struggled valiantly around the windy end of the island. The plastic slickers were coming in handy against the spray as the boat pitched and tossed in the late afternoon wind. They were soaking wet before they gained the low caves, which were hidden on the windward side of the island.

When they reached the lee of one of the caves, the wind stopped suddenly, and they were able to communicate their report to a heavy-set man, waiting for them in another low flat boat such as Tunisian fishermen use.

He was unhappy with their report. Product was not flowing as had been originally planned, and the work on the two chemical sites had been fraught with unexplained delays. He told them both that if progress wasn't made, and soon, on beginning to export the quantities expected, they would no longer be in the employ of the "company."

Von Grantz and his aide were of a generation of Germans who buckled under the slightest show of authority. They became still and white faced under the operatives threats. They had heard what happened to men who were no longer in the employ of the "company", they quietly disappeared and were never heard from again.

Chapter Ten

Rick pushed the jeep as hard as it would go over the washboard roads. Here and there, he hit a patch of pure sand, which gave a moment's relief from the jarring on his kidneys, but also offered the constant threat of the Jeep being bogged down and his having to stop to shovel the vehicle out.

The road was dusty and hot and it was frustrating to retrace his steps and lose more time. But he was more and more convinced that Robbie's trail led to Algeria, and that the police chief in Touzeur might know more than he was telling. It was a least worth a chance. He passed the place where he had encountered the Arab on the Harley. Seeing no trace of the bike or the body, he smiled ruefully. The desert was quick to claim its own and the Harley was probably now displayed outside some nomad's tent, as a place to hang the washing.

The air was turning dusty and yellow, and it tasted gritty between his teeth when he stopped for a lunch of canned sardines, bread and cheese, the wayfarers basic food. He swigged it down with some water, which already tasted of gasoline. He had added two large tanks of water, along with his extra gas. It smelled as though one had leaked into the other.

By the time he reached Tozeur the sand was shifting across the road, almost obliterating it. He saw the tall palm trees of the oasis before he saw the town. The buildings of mud brick were the same color as the sand, which now swirled through the air.

He pulled up in front of the police station, where several men, who looked as though they should be locked up inside, lounged around on the steps drinking tea from tiny black cups. Or perhaps the cups were clear and the tea was black. It was hard to tell. As he passed by, they mumbled a greeting in his direction and continued languidly swatting flies and sipping tea.

The police chief looked up from his cluttered desk and greeted him like an old friend. He gestured Rick into a sheepskin covered chair. Rick sat, lounging like a man who has all the time in the world. He was remembering that you don't get anywhere in the Arab world with haste. But it was hard to shake off the habits of American business. He took a deep breath and waited for the chief to speak first, which he did.

"So my friend, you have come back to Tozeur. Is it the taste of our dates that have drawn you?"

Rick nodded, "When mixed with your local sand, they are unforgettable."

The Chief smiled, showing strong white teeth in his creased face. His black eyes narrowed. "You are seeking you son still, yes? Well, Allah has been good to you. I have news."

Rick gripped the edge of the table. Keeping his face noncommittal. "What news?" he asked, already preparing himself to hear that Robbie was dead.

The man looked at Rick almost kindly. "It is not what you fear. But that may not be for long. Your son is being 'entertained' by a group of bandits who live in the hills across the border. They make periodic raids into our part of the desert to steal sheep or whatever else they can find." He spit on the floor and took a sip of his tea. "We caught one of them and he told us about the American boy in their camp. He wanted to trade the information for his freedom."

"And did he?" Rick asked.

"It was not convenient", the chief replied with a slight grimace. But if you want to find your son I will send a man with you 'under cover' as you say. We would like to put some fear into these men. They are becoming too arrogant and what they do is against the Koran."

"Would he have trouble getting across the border?"

"No more than you would alone my friend. These things can be arranged, *ensh'allah*. The crossing to El Owed is one of the most popular tourist crossings, even in these troubled times." He eased his girth out of the chair. "I will send a man with you this evening, these things are best done quickly and under the cover of darkness."

When Rick saw the police chief a few hours later he was standing beside a thin young man with dark skin and high cheekbones dressed in a geleba and baggy trousers. He touched his heart and his forehead in greeting and said in accented English, "Brahim is my name." On his head he wore a small multicolored cap set at a rakish angle.

The young man was ready to jump into the Jeep, but the chief put a restraining hand on his shoulder." He is *Fezzani* and speaks the language of the desert. His task is to locate these people for us and to help you bargain for your son if necessary. In exchange I wish you both to return with evidence of these bandits which I can use to keep them and their merchandise out of my country."

"Does he have papers to get us across?" Rick asked.

"He has papers if you have Algerian Dinars. If not there is a bank in Bou Arona just across the border. You must take at least one thousand dinars in with you each at the government exchange rate. What you can exchange at the black market rate once you get in is up to you."

Rick smiled grimly. " Sounds as if this is an all expenses paid vocation for Brahim. I hope he's worth the investment," he said, starting the Jeep's motor.

The chief raised his voice over the sound of the motor. "Since you have very little chance of locating your son with out him. You may find that he is worth it. Be back in three days. You have short term visas."

The sky was darkening. Brahim's plan was to drive to Nefta to reconnoiter and ask questions and then to cross the border just before the last call to prayer. At this time the guards were more apt to be busy with their devotions and less apt to be suspicious of an American tourist and his Tunisian guide.

Rick's skepticism grew as the Tunisian grew more enthusiastic about his plan. But one thing was sure. He probably had more chance of finding Robbie with someone who knew this part of the country and the desert. Brahim came from the desert and for centuries his people had wandered across the face of the *Magreb* herding their animals with no thought of country or of border. The drawing of an arbitrary line by European powers had made him a Tunisian rather than an Algerian. Rick knew this, Brahim didn't. The young policeman was simply looking forward to an adventure and the chance to prove himself.

They reached Nefta just before dusk. The town was even dustier than Tozeur. But a small oasis and a grand tourist hotel on the hill gave it a certain cachet. Rick filled the tanks with gas and water while Brahim chatted idly with some men at a sidewalk cafe. Rick watched him curiously. The young man had an ingenious air and a rapid way of speaking which seemed to put people at ease. He soon had the old men chatting and *hamdulla-ing* and shaking their toothless heads.

Rick paid for the gas and waited impatiently to leave. Brahim's conversation seemed to have degenerated into a purely social one. He was now waving his arms as if in the midst of a particularly hair raising story. When Rick, playing the American tourist, honked the horn and gestured him to the car, he came reluctantly.

He slid onto the scorching seat of the Jeep and looked at Rick reproachfully out of eyes as black as olives. His anger made him forget his English. But the gist of it was the Rick was never to honk at him again in public. He was not a servant but an agent of the police doing his duty. Besides the old men had given his useful information.

"Which Was?" Rick asked impatiently, putting the jeep into gear and stepping on the accelerator. Which resulted in a cloud of dust enveloping them as they left Nefta behind.

"Just as my Chief has been told. There are two or perhaps three gangs operating here and further south. They make raids on the towns to kill and take what they can and then escape back into the desert. The people here are afraid that soon they will become more daring and come into Tunisia. They don't have to much protection down here." He lapsed into a thoughtful silence, watching the road.

"And" Rick prompted. "Did he say anything about an American boy?"

Brahim looked thoughtful. "One of them brags that he has a new blonde boy which he keeps to entertain him, hoping for ransom. But they do not know where this one is. He comes like a sandstorm and then disappears."

"How do these toothless old men know such things. "Rick asked angrily, driving his foot harder onto the gas pedal.

Brahim looked at him almost with pity. "The sands never stop whispering and the sands know everything," he said, and then lapsed into silence.

They reached the border just before the time for prayers. As Brahim had predicted, the guards were too preoccupied to pay more than cursory attention to their papers. It seemed that the police chief had done his work well. And the small gift of Tunisian dinars also helped to grease the wheels of progress. Rick had a sufficient amount of both US dollars and Tunisian and Algerian Dinars to pay his way out of most predicaments should the need arise. He had learned this from his earlier trips to the Arab world. He kept these in several places where they would not be discovered easily.

Brahim chatted easily with the border guards. Bragging about the American tourist he had in tow, Rick surmised. At any rate the ruse seemed to work for the moment and they left the guards prostrating themselves towards Mecca and saying their prayers as the Jeep lurched forward into the desert.

"We should stop for the night somewhere in the desert before we reach El Owed", Brahim suggested. "They may look more carefully at our papers once they have said their prayers."

Rick agreed. Now that they were in Algeria he wanted to start out across the desert in the direction in which Robbie has last been seen. It was a temptation to try to do this at night. But he knew that the sands were treacherous and one broken axle could mean a long trek back on foot.

Brahim seemed content to parallel the road for a while until they found a rocky outcropping banked with sand which provided some protection from curious border guards. Nevertheless Rick slept fitfully with his pistol strapped to his side. He dreamed again of Robbie and this time the feeling of fear he got from the boy was so real that he woke shaking and covered with sweat.

It was about midnight. The sky had cleared and the stars looked so close that it seemed you could reach up and touch them. He sat for a while thinking, willing himself to be calm and to think rationally. Time was clearly running out. If he didn't find Robbie in the next few days, it would be over. He looked over at Brahim, sleeping soundly wrapped in his geleba and a tattered blanket. He looked not much older then Robbie. And again Rick felt a tinge of fear. What if it was already too late. What if his son was lost forever. He felt the cold pistol at his side and knew that if Robbie wasn't alive, his kidnapers would die also with as much pain as he could inflict.

* * *

Janine wanted to avoid having dinner at all. The silence from her operative in D'Jerba was becoming oppressive. The longer she waited to see what had happened, the greater chance she was taking with the whole operation. Von Grantz and his aide had returned from their afternoon adventure and secreted themselves in their room. Janine went to find them, hoping to get a clue as to their whereabouts and also to escape being alone with Ahmed, whose glances were becoming increasingly erotic.

She found them huddled in their room sharing a large bottle of schnapps. Von Grantz was not his usual immaculate self and his assistant had passed beyond the point of no return. They declined dinner, saying that they had work to do. Janine was left on her own to deal with Ahmed. She was able to get rid of him only by promising to meet him in town for dinner at a famous tourist spot, the Restaurant Aladdin. She hoped the delay would give him time to cool his ardor and also give her time to go into town first and see if she could find out what had happened to her counterpart in D'Jerba.

She dressed conservatively in a dark dress with long sleeves and covered her hair with a scarf. Even though the Tunisians were very used to tourists she didn't want to be confused with a French woman looking for a date with one of the handsome beach boys who thronged the town.

She gave the taxi driver a false address on the other side of the souk from where she knew the operative lived. Walking quickly through the crowds she zig zagged back and forth through the winding streets, stopping now and then to examine something in a shop and watching her back to make sure that she wasn't being followed.

When she was sure that she was alone and shielded by the crowds she approached the street where the operative lived. His address was on a narrow street lined with square, one story white houses with wooden doors and no windows on the street. His house was two story which was its only identifying feature. The roof was flat and for a moment she thought that she saw movement above. Then she heard a low mournful wailing and a black cat peered down at her over the edge of the roof. It spat and hissed as if daring her to knock.

Seeing no-one on the street except three small boys playing in the dust at the end of the road, she knocked quietly and then harder. There was no reply. No sound came from within. The cat, having done it's guard duty had disappeared. Janine knocked again and when there was still no answer, tried the knob. It was heavy in her hand and turned with difficulty. But the door swung open, slowly with a creaking sound. Inside there was only blackness and a strange sweet smell. She closed the door behind her and stood for a moment letting her eyes become accustomed to the darkness.

It was a typical D'Jerban house with tile floors and elaborately painted wooden tables low to the ground. Someone had added a touch of sophistication in a computer which blinked at her from the corner of the room. The rug was a good one from Kerowan. By the light of the computer screen she could see that there was a large stain on one corner of it, which she had at first taken to be a shadow. She moved cautiously forward.

A shadow bounded at her screaming and landed on her back. It was the cat, still angry and trying to defend her territory. Janine lost her balance and fell to one knee. It was then that she saw it. What she had taken to be another rug rolled in the corner of the room was a man. His hands tied behind his back and his throat cut from ear to ear.

Janine gagged, knowing now what was the source of the sickly sweet smell. It was his life's blood soaking the carpet. He clutched something in his hand. It was a scrap of paper with something written in Arabic script and badly smeared with his blood. Whoever had done this must have been in such a hurry to get away that they hadn't bothered to remove it. Or maybe they didn't care. Janine knew that she had taken a big risk coming here, both for herself and for the agency. It was important that she keep her cover as a Commercial Attaché for the embassy. Finding and reporting this murder to the authorities was something she couldn't afford to do.

She took the bloody piece of paper from her contact's cold and lifeless fist and put it in her purse. Then she covered the body with the rug, gagging again as she did so. The computer bothered her. Why hadn't the murderer turned it off or smashed it so that no files could be retrieved? She found a disk and programmed the machine to download its files. While this was being done she looked carefully in the other two rooms. Nothing was disturbed. Whoever had done this had come deliberately to do murder and not even bothered to cover their tracks by trying to make it look like a robbery. Leaving a valuable computer was evidence enough of that.

When she was sure that the files had been downloaded and then deleted, she switched the computer off and got ready to leave the room in the dark. Before she could cross the room the door began to swing open slowly, flooding the doorway with late afternoon sunshine.

She turned quickly to see if the body was hidden. It looked like a pile of rugs in the corner. Except for the sickly sweet smell there was no other evidence of a murder. She turned back to see Ahmed's body filling the doorway. The expression on his face was hidden by the blinding sun behind him.

She walked quickly toward him. Her only thought to get him away before he became too curious and began to look around the room. She stood in front of him and put on her most provocative smile. "I guess that I could ask you what you are doing here. Or do you always follow your dinner dates to make sure that they make it on time?"

"Only if they come alone to dangerous parts of town," he said, standing his ground in the doorway. "What would an embassy lady like you be doing here?"

Janine thought fast. "But I am also a student of architecture. I was told that this house was an ancient *fundug* or pilgrim house, and that the man who owned it might be willing to show it to me. He seems to be not here at the moment, even though I made an appointment."

Ahmed seemed to consider her explanation carefully. But he remained in the doorway. Janine moved closer to him, trying to pull the heavy door closed behind her as she did. The officer still did not move. Now she was so close to him that she could feel his breath on her face. He smiled knowingly and reached behind her, pulling her closer to him. Only the openness of the street and his Arab modesty kept him from pulling her into his arms. But that could wait until later.

Now he knew that she was covering something and that she would pay whatever he wanted to keep it a secret. He could return to the house later to find what it was hiding. He had the pretty American woman in a vise which could close slowly in a time of his own choosing. He smiled charmingly and gestured her into the street. First they would have dinner.

*   *   *

The report on von Grantz's activities, or lack of them, was already on Claude Bonet's desk. He looked at these reports the last thing each evening after his secretary had gone home. It was his secret pleasure to look at a map of the *Magreb* which was hidden behind a wall mirror in his office and which turned electronically to show all of his companies legitimate activities in that part of the world. By pressing a secret button other lights appeared. These were the covert activities which he kept for himself.

Even Duke Weston didn't know about these. The profits from them came directly into Bonet's pockets, even though all of the products were developed from by-products of legitimate business deals. These clandestine operations were netting him millions. The little boy who had lived on bread and onions was now in a position to wipe out the entire population of Algeria if he so desired.

But von Grantz was not doing his job, Bonet reflected as he lit a Gauloise and drew in the black smoke appreciatively. These East Germans had no guts. They had lived too long under Communism. It had killed both their work ethic and their imagination. They had lost the ability to improvise. The project in Tunisia was only a small part of a much larger scheme. But if the chemicals did not move from there in a timely manner it held up the whole operation in Libya and Algeria and ultimately Iraq.

As the pungent smoke drifted upward, he imagined himself in full control of North Africa. Weston still had too many American scruples. He didn't mind trading illegally with countries which were off limits. But one whiff of the poison gas scheme and he would scream like a cut bull. But Weston too could be eliminated as well as his grandson and his daughter. He buzzed his secretary and left a message for the morning. He wanted his private jet ready to leave for D'Jerba in the morning. The time had come to take things into his own hands.

*   *   *

Melanie was getting tired of Tunis. She had shopped the gold and perfume markets in the Souk in the company of a long suffering Embassy wife whose job it was to look after official visitors. The Ambassador had given them his car and chauffeur today, which was unusual. But his wife was in Paris for a few days and he was very grateful to get Duke Weston's daughter out of his hair. As far as he was concerned she was a spoiled rich man's daughter who had come to Tunisia for the sole purpose of making his life miserable and interfering with his tennis games.

It was unheard of that she should just be left to fend for herself in an Arab county. Besides Washington had made it clear that she was to be extended "every courtesy". Which meant that half his staff and most of the wives had taken turns entertaining her since Mrs. Olgelvie had departed for Paris the day after the infamous dinner party.

When Melanie was bored, she shopped. She had bought numerous bird cages in Sidi Bou Said, a dozen Kairouan rugs from various merchants and she was now in the process of cleaning out the gold and silver markets. There was no word of Robbie and also no news of Rick. It was as if they had both dropped off the face of the earth. He father said only that he "was working on it from his end" and advised her to stay put, keep putting pressure on the Ambassador and wait in Tunis for news. But no news came.

While she was trying on a gold wedding necklace which looked like finely wrought gold lace, she had an inspiration. Why not go south and look for Robbie herself. The handsome young embassy Attaché had said that the party was heading to D'Jerba. There were beaches there and several nice resorts he said. There might even be a few interesting

European men. At least it would be doing something. Better than waiting around. "I'll take two", she told the gold merchant, precipitously and without bargaining. The Embassy wife looked horrified and the gold merchant looked disappointed.

As much as he enjoyed selling jewelry, he enjoyed negotiating the price. Anyone who paid the first price asked did not understand the game. It was close to an insult.

Now that she had a plan Melanie felt better. She would fly to D'Jerba in the morning. What's more, she would ask the Ambassador to send Brian the preppie young attaché with her as an escort. Certainly she couldn't be expected to run around the country by herself. She needed a certain amount of protection. Besides the young officer was most attractive in a clean cut, southern sort of way. He might be amusing to have around for a few days. And at least she would be where she would get the first news of Robbie if any were to come. Yes, D'Jerba was the place to go tomorrow.

Ambassador Olgelvie was more than happy to have news of Melanie's departure for D'Jerba. The loss of a junior officer for a few days was a small price to pay for some peace and quiet and a chance to catch up on his tennis and other pursuits while his wife was away. There was that attractive young secretary in decoding. Might be just the time to get off some of his classified documents to Washington.

Brian Scott the third, took the news much less calmly. Since he had been assigned to Tunisia as his first post in the Arab world he had had some curious assignments. An on call fourth for bridge at the Ambassador's residence; arriving early and passing the peanuts at residence parties. He had even been asked to hide out at the front of the Residence before dinner parties and signal the arrival of guests of honor. He looked upon accompanying Melanie to D'Jerba with decidedly mixed emotions.

On the one hand she was an attractive female but decidedly out of reach because of her Washington connections. On the other hand he had not yet been to D'Jerba and the experience might be fun. But for a young man from The University of Virginia with an advanced degree in classical Arabic, he felt that his talents so far had been decidedly underused by the Foreign Service.

But he knew Olgelvie well enough not to show his discomfort. His one year efficiency report was to be written in the next few months. Cooperation and being a team player were highly prized in the Foreign Service. In fact they seemed to rank higher than his skills in classical Arabic and the culture of the region which where unquestionable.

He sighed as he packed his overnight bag with the requisite khaki pants and navy blue jacket which had been his uniform since his undergraduate days. Fortunately they always looked well on his slender blonde frame. His eyes were pale blue and looked out earnestly from steel rimmed glasses. His hair was sandy and worn slightly long. All in all he looked like someone's preppie son. So far a number of women at the post had tried to adopt him. Which ones had succeeded only he knew for sure, and he kept his counsel. A Virginia gentleman always did. It was in the genes.

He hoped that Melanie's plans did not include baking in the sun for too long. His pale skin freckled and then turned the color of an angry turkey wattle as his granny used to say. Southern women did not look kindly on to much sun. Which was one of the reasons that she had preserved a classic beauty even into old age.

Melanie, on the other hand, was already packing several bikinis which even she had had the good sense not to wear around the Ambassador's pool. She was looking forward to D'Jerba, not only for the companionship of the boyish foreign service officer, but also to get away from the Embassy wives whose company she had begun to find boring and oppressive. She packed enough clothes for at least a month, adding some of the gelabas she had found 'amusing' in the market. There was one fuschia and gold one that she found especially attractive.

The phone rang and Brian's voice on the other end told her that he was waiting downstairs in the car. The plane to D'Jerba was at ten o'clock and there was just one this morning. She heard the edge of impatience in his usually languid southern voice and smiled. She enjoyed keeping men waiting. In fact, she had raised it to an art. "I'll be down in a minute darling", she cooed into the phone. Then she went into the bathroom and spent another ten minutes on her hair, until there was a knock on her door. She opened it to find Brian and an Embassy chauffeur waiting outside to take her bags. Melanie sailed out of the room delighted. Now she had two men waiting on her.

Brian stood straighter and followed her down the stairs, ignoring the amused glances of the hotel staff. As he did so, he vowed to get even with this mannerless Yankee. He didn't yet know how or when. But the great grandson of Brian Lee Scott the first, hero of the battle of Richmond, was not going to be treated in this manner.

Chapter Eleven

Rick woke from a cold dark sleep. It was barely light and the desert lay as though under water, sky and land blending together in a soft blue haze. A few feet away Brahim was already awake, making tea in a small pot over a fire of twigs and humming softly to himself. Rick watched him silently for a moment. The young man looked cheerful, fully concentrating on his task. Rick wondered if he had ever felt that carefree or happy in his life. If so, it was too long ago to remember.

Brahim saw him watching and offered him a cup of tea and a husk of bread which he pulled out of his flowing garment. Rick accepted gratefully. The hot sweet liquid with its sharp aftertaste of tannin seared his tongue and made him ready to face the day.

"So what now?" he asked the young Arab policeman. "Which way do we go in this trackless wasteland to find my son?"

Brahim munched on his bread reflectively. He squatted on his heels with his robe spread around him, his eyes opaque. "I do not know, no one knows. We can only go into the desert and let them find us", as he squinted toward the horizon. "Even now they may be watching us. It is their custom to know everything, to watch everything. The desert is their home, not ours."

"But you come from desert people," Rick protested. "That is why the chief sent you with me."

Brahim smiled and shook his head. "He sent me to make sure that you do not get into trouble or make trouble with the Algerian police. Whether or not we find you son makes no difference to him", he paused and looked around, "but it does to me. I hate these bandits and what they do to my people. They steal from everyone even the most poor. If a family has only one sheep, they take it. Only one son, they steal him to fight, and with the daughters, they do worse. He stood up, straightening his gelaba. "I will lead you to where these ones can find you. What you do with them is your business, not mine."

They covered their small fire and packed their few belongings into the Jeep. Brahim pointed out a track which led deeper into the desert and to the south of El Oued. In the distance Rick could see the haze of mountains and tall rocky outcroppings that seemed to grow directly out of the land, as if thrust up centuries ago by a giant upheaval. The track was in deep sand and several times they just avoided being stuck. Each time this happened, Brahim insisted that they get out and look around and that Rick take some pictures of him against the mountains. This was supposedly to maintain their tourist cover, but Rick began to wonder if Brahim was just into having photographs of himself on this 'secret' mission.

By noon the sun was blistering, there was no shade in sight and Rick's patience had worn almost to the breaking point. He drove the Jeep grimly on, refusing to stop, jolting over the rocks and sand with his eyes on the distant hills which seemed never to get any closer. His eyes were gritty with sand under his sunglasses. There was sand in his mouth and in the sweat that poured down his face. After an axles' wrenching jolt he stopped the Jeep for a minute to check underneath and to wash his face with the gasoline scented water. Brahim, who had been asleep in the back seat, suggested that they have lunch in the shade of the Jeep and take their bearings.

"Of what?", Rick asked testily. "Sand, rocks and sun as far as the eye can see and that's about all."

"Except for this" Brahim answered, turning over what looked like a brown rock with his foot. Underneath it was a lighter brown color and texture. "This is horse dung and it is not very old. It is not yet completely dried out. Whoever is riding this horse is not far away. They may even have been watching us."

"How far can a horse travel in this desert in a day?"

"Thirty or forty miles", Brahim answered. "They are desert horses, bred for endurance. But they must have water, so they go towards the mountains."

"And so shall we," Rick answered, climbing back into the Jeep and putting it in gear. "I want to reach those mountains by dusk. Either we will find the bandits or let them find us first. It doesn't much matter now. Time is running out, for both me and my son."

*   *   *

Janine and Ahmed reached the restaurant just after sunset. He had led her through the winding streets without talking but with a set to his shoulders that looked like a man who had made up his mind about something. Janine walked silently beside him thinking through her cover story carefully. It was important that she not slip up, and even more important that she report to the Embassy immediately what she had found. The death of the D'Jerba operative was not the work of a trained professional. Or if it was, it had been deliberately planned to put her, or whoever found him, off guard.

She followed Ahmed into the restaurant still busy with her thoughts. Once settled at a low table surrounded by cushions and lit by a many faceted brass lamp which threw ornate shadows on the wall, she excused herself to go to the ladies room. Ahmed watched her as she walked toward the back of the restaurant, letting his eyes roam speculatively over her departing figure.

Once inside the privacy of the ladies room, Janine locked the door, pulled her cellular phone from her bag and dialed a number to be used only in case of code one emergencies. This rang directly into the Ambassador's residence, and was only answered by him or by a special recording machine. The machine answered and she gave her report succinctly, watching all the while to make sure than no one tried the door. She asked specifically for backup since Rick had not accompanied her to D'Jerba.

"That should cheat the old man out of one of his tennis games", she thought as she replaced the phone in her bag. Then she applied lipstick and splashed rosewater on her hands and face before she dared to leave the security of the ladies room. The sickly sweet smell of the dead man's rotting flesh still seemed to cling to her clothes and hair. She moistened her hair with rosewater and clipped it up with a comb from her purse. She was delaying the moment when she had to face Ahmed again. She knew that he suspected something and that he was playing dumb to lull her into a false sense of security. However, at the moment he was the only ally she had. If he was indeed a real ally.

She knew that the Tunisian military were deeply divided since the Conservative Arab party had been banned from elections. The trouble in, Algeria with all the crimes done in the name of Arab unity, had only made the situation more difficult for those who were even slightly sympathetic with the goals of *An Nahda*. She suspected that Ahmed might be one of these. But allegiances changed quickly in this part of the world. It was better to keep playing her hand alone as long as she was able.

She smiled as she walked back into the dining room which was slowly filling with a variety of nationalities on vacation on this sun drenched island. The women were smartly, if casually, dressed and the men wore a variety of European and Arab garb. She heard a great deal of French and some German being spoken as she made her way back to the table in the corner that Ahmed had chosen. A bottle of French wine was cooling on the table. The officer was leaning back on the cushions, his eyes half-closed as he listened to the undulating whine of the Tunisian music.

"Do you understand the words?" he asked her as she sank into the pillows across from him, in what she hoped was a graceful manner.

"I have some Arabic, enough to catch a word here and there", she replied as he filled her glass with a dry white wine.

"It is a most beautiful language. There are over one hundred words alone to describe a lion and even more to describe love. We Arabs are a very inventive people when it comes to love", he said, eyeing her appreciatively.

"So I have heard," Janine replied, looking at him over the rim of her glass. There was no harm in appearing to flirt with him here in a roomful of people. The problem would come when he got her back to the hotel. She could probably out-run him, but he out-weighed her and out-muscled her, that was for certain.

"Tell me about you colleague Harrison? Where is he and have you heard from him", he asked, sipping his wine and reaching idly for her hand.

"He will join us in a day or so", Janine replied. "He had business of his own to attend to."

"As relates to his son?"

"I believe so," Janine replied, grateful that the conversation had taken this neutral turn.

"If the boy is caught in Tunisia, he will probably be tried and convicted of drug dealing. Unless your Embassy makes a special intervention for him and gets him out of the country immediately. Is your Ambassador prepared to do that?"

Janine shrugged. "Who knows what the Ambassador will do. It would be his decision."

"But his grandfather is a very powerful man. Is he not? The kind of man for whom your Ambassador might be moved to use his influence with our President to pardon the boy."

"If he is found and if he is guilty." Janine said casually, withdrawing her hand. "Can we order dinner? I'm starving."

As they were finishing their meal, Melanie and Brian Scott entered the restaurant fresh from their tour of the island. Melanie was dusty and grim and young Brian was longing for a scotch and a hot bath and some blessed time away from Melanie. He spied Janine as she was leaving and greeted her like an old friend.

Ahmed watched her suspiciously while Janine smiled in delight, thanking her lucky stars. The intervention of these two Americans put quite another light on the evening. She introduced Ahmed, whose expression changed as he examined Melanie more closely. Melanie, always glad for a new man to conquer, fluttered her eyelashes and gave the handsome Arab her hand. "Don't leave so early," she pleaded. "Do stay and have at least one glass of wine with us. We don't know anybody in D'Jerba." This was said with the same petulant pout of her rosy lips that had always worked on her father.

"Oh yes, lets do," Janine insisted, hoping for a few private words with Brian, who looked decidedly relieved to have Melanie's attention turned elsewhere for the moment. He ran a hand through his tousled hair, cleaned his dusty glasses, and looked inquiringly through them at Janine.

"So how is your fact finding trip going?" he asked innocently. Taking a glass from the tray offered by the obsequious waiter.

"I've found a few more facts than I expected," Janine replied softly, watching Ahmed look deep into Melanie's blue eyes while she giggled up at him.

"Where is Harrison?", Brian asked.

Janine shrugged. "It's anybody's guess. At any rate he hasn't been much help. Too involved with personal difficulties I guess."

The young officer nodded. It offended his Southern sensibilities to see Janine abandoned in the middle of a mission. And he had taken an immediate dislike to the Arab officer, even if he was doing him the favor of taking Melanie off his hands for a little while.

"Where are you staying?", Janine asked casually.

"Probably here. Why?"

"Why don't you come back to the other side of the island with us. The swimming is better and then we could all be together in the same hotel." Janine said with real enthusiasm. Melanie could keep Ahmed busy while she used Brian to help find out what was going on. It would be good to have someone that she could trust on her side. And from what she had seen of the junior officer he was straight arrow all the way.

It was easy to get Melanie to go along with the idea. Several glasses of wine had done their work. She was essentially a social creature and had long since run out of conversation with Brian. The young officer was determined to be polite but not intimate with her on any count. He had his future in the Foreign Service to think of. And there was no way that Duke Weston's daughter could bring him anything but trouble.

They took two small taxies back to their hotel. Janine managed to put Melanie in with Ahmed so that she could share with Brian. On the bouncing ride she told him all that she thought was wise about the mission. But she warned him to keep his eyes on Ahmed and on the two Germans they were traveling with. She also told him that for the moment she was out of contact with the Embassy so they were operating pretty much on their own.

Brian's eyes lighted up. This sounded like cloak and dagger stuff. The kind of thing he had hoped to get involved in. He could tell that Janine wasn't telling him the whole story and this only wetted his appetite for more. Whatever was involved it was a whole lot more fun than baby sitting Melanie for the weekend and he told Janine so, fixing her with his earnest blue eyes, and warming her with his Southern accent.

By the time they arrived at their hotel and unpacked Melanie's copious luggage, Janine and Brian were acting like comrades under arms. Ahmed had swept Duke Weston's daughter off to take an evening swim in the pool. Brian and Janine could hear them splashing and talking and then there was a long and meaningful silence.

"Saved by the bell", Janine thought to herself as she wished Brian good night, resisting his efforts to wangle more information out of her.

She had told him just enough to whet his appetite and get him on her side, without revealing anything that it would be dangerous for him to know should he be questioned.

Janine locked her door and pulled the curtains so that no one could see in. Then she tried the Ambassador's private number again, and again got an answering machine. The two Germans were conspicuous by their absence. There were no lights from their rooms and the boy who cleaned the rooms said that they had not been in for dinner.

Janine turned out her lights and sat silently in the darkness for a long time before she got sleepy. She could hear the sounds of splashing in the pool and of some of the other guests calling to each other. She wondered if during the night Ahmed would come knocking at her door. She loaded her pistol and put it under her pillow before she finally closed her eyes to sleep.

*   *   *

Claude Bonet's private jet arrived in D'Jerba at one A.M. The airport was deserted except for a skeleton crew alerted to welcome the plane and get Bonet to his villa on the other side of the island. He found it amusing to keep these retreats at strategic points throughout the world. He could arrive at any of them unannounced and find them always exquisitely appointed and stocked with his favorite wines. Well paid retainers kept them waiting at all times. It gave him a sense of power to have influence over so many lives; to have so many people depending on him and to know that he could sever the relationships at any time.

He was not well liked, but he was respected and he was powerful. For a poor boy from the mountains of Algeria, this was all a solace to his soul. If he had one, which was sometimes a matter of dispute to the men who worked for him. Bonet had only male employees. He disliked women, did not trust them, and refused to have them in his employ unless absolutely necessary. His motherly, gray-haired, secretary was the only exception.

This had caused some talk in the beginning. But now he was so powerful and successful that gossips put it down to his eccentric millionaire ways. Those who thought of it at all surmised that there might be a sexual preference involved, and didn't really care.

Bonet made it a habit to occasionally be seen with the world's most beautiful women on his arm for one public function or another when necessary. Now he was angry and hungry. This simple mission in D'Jerba was taking more than its allotted time and each day the prospect of profit from it got less secure. The Germans were not reliable and all kinds of other people had gotten involved to muddy the waters. He intended to clean up the mess himself or at least make sure that certain heads would roll before he left the island.

As his limousine pulled into the desert night toward his villa, he seemed to be unobserved. However, this was never the case in the Arab world. A gelaba clad figure stepped out of the shadows and trotted after the car until it was out of sight. Then Ahmed walked slowly back to the hotel and crawled back into bed without waking the sleeping Melanie.

The next morning the beach was littered with half sleeping bodies drinking up the morning sun when Bonet's chauffeur arrived with lunch invitations for Melanie and her companions. She fluttered her eyes, and her pouter pigeon chest swelled with this evidence of her importance. "Daddy must have sent him to look after me", she told the assembled beach party. "He's a charming man and one of daddy's oldest friends." Janine made gagging motions in the direction of the young Southern officer who grinned back at her impishly.

"Well I for one would like to see how he lives," Brian answered. "Rumor has it that his villa is a showplace and that he has some wonderful antiques collected from all over the Arab world."

"You mean stolen," Janine muttered. But she too was anxious to make contact with Bonet and see how he fitted into this puzzle. If she got a good lunch in the process, well then so much the better.

The villa was indeed breathtaking. Set on the edge of the sea, it was surrounded by ancient olive trees, the sand stone walls covered with flame colored bougainvillea. Inside was a deceptively simple Arab house built around a central courtyard which contained a limpid blue swimming pool with a fountain in the center, surrounded by rare tropical plants. Bonet greeted them as they arrived, his silver blonde hair was cut in military fashion and his eyes were opaque gray under eyebrows which were almost white. He wore a white linen coat and trousers and a turquoise silk shirt which accentuated his coloring.

He was conscious of the effect he had upon Melanie and less sure of it upon Janine. But he took both of their arms and led them into the shadowed villa, one on either side. Like a prince eager to show off his private realm.

Janine reacted almost viscerally at the touch of his hand on her arm. His fingers were ice cold even though the day was by now very warm. He held on to her hand tightly as he showed her around the room, seemingly anxious to show off his treasures of Arab pottery and embroidered calligraphy. The pressure of his fingers was intense. When she tried to pull away he tightened his grip and smiled at her revealing perfect white teeth. "Doesn't your State Department encourage you to learn about Arab art and culture?" He said in a voice that just escaped being menacing.

"I think that the lady has seen all that she wishes", Ahmed answered from the other side of the room, where he had been watching the scene unfold. There was an unmistakable note of menace in his voice. Melanie laughed, breaking the spell. "Well, if I don't get something cold to drink right away, I'm going to faint right here in your living room", she said, fluttering her eyes at Bonet, and letting go of his hand.

"Of course," he answered, releasing Janine's arm for a moment to clap his hands. An Arab servant appeared out of the shadows with a tray of cool iced drinks. Janine took the opportunity to move to the other side of the room near the young Southerner. Brian put his hand on her arm as she moved toward him. He didn't like the looks of this fellow Bonet. There was something false about him and this whole setup. He hoped that Melanie would keep her head. He didn't like the idea of having to flush her out of this Frenchman's clutches later on this evening. He was beginning to wish that he had stayed in his quiet cubbyhole of an office in Tunis.

The lunch was leisurely and served in the shade of the veranda with the tinkling sound of the fountain making cool music in the background. Bonet now seemed to be intent upon playing the role of the attentive host, with Melanie to his right and Janine to his left. Ahmed and Brian sat near the end of the table, just far enough away not to be able to hear Bonet's whispered asides to Melanie as he kept her glass filled with a dry sparkling wine.

Janine sat rigidly beside him. She returned his compliments with a nod of her head or a dismissive wave of her hand and concentrated on the various courses set before her. There was a clear cold soup to start and then a delicious Tunisian *Brique,* crispy with spiced meat and egg inside. This was followed by an excellent cous-cous with highly seasoned lamb and eggplant. Then ice cold melon, and finally sweet mint tea with tiny pinenut meats floating in it. Each course was served with an appropriate wine and by the time they were finished Melanie was giggling slightly and leaning provocatively on Bonet's shoulder.

Ahmed rose stiffly to his feet as soon as the tea was served. He complimented Bonet on the excellent meal and then asked to be excused, moving around the table to take Melanie's arm to help her rise from the table. But Melanie was in her cups and she held out her hand to Bonet playfully. "I want to swim now," she said, ogling him with her wide blue eyes. "Take off all my clothes and swim in your nice pool with you."

Bonet smiled over at Janine. " Only if your friend will join us," he said, with what passed for a smile. "A blond and a brunette for desert, how delicious."

Janine saw Ahmed make a movement which telegraphed that he was armed and ready to go for the Frenchman. She stepped in front of him, deflecting the gesture. The cords in his neck stood out hard with anger. The young Southerner intervened just in time, putting a hand under Melanie's arm and helping her to her feet. "Let's all swim back at the hotel after lunch," he said cheerfully. Perhaps Mr. Bonet will join us after we've all slept off this excellent lunch." He moved a protesting Melanie towards the door, all the while keeping up a cheerful banter. Falling back on a technique he had learned at fraternity parties at the University of Virginia, which now stood him in good stead.

Janine followed him to the door blessing his Southern upbringing. Ahmed had not moved from his position of confrontation with Bonet. His arm had relaxed a bit but his stance said that he longed to finish the effete Frenchman. Bonet smiled and followed the rest of them to the door. He knew that the Arab would not risk creating an incident over so small a matter. What he did not know was that he had just created a subtle and dangerous enemy in the person of Captain Ahmed Haddad.

Chapter Twelve

By nightfall Rick was more tired and thirsty than he ever remembered being in his life. The distant mountains looked no closer, although they had been moving toward them all day. Brahim had fallen into a morose silence. He had slept most of the afternoon, fallen into a sort of desert swoon that it seemed no amount of jogging could rouse him from. There was no road, only a rock strewn path which disappeared from time to time into a *waddi* with no trace of water. Only the sight of the blue mountains in the distance kept them going, and the promise of sundown.

In the rational part of his mind, Rick acknowledged that this was probably a wild goose chase. Some kind of emotional journey motivated only by the fact that he was doing something about Robbie and not just leaving it all to fate. He knew how slim his chances were of finding anything in this blasted desert. And that what he did find might just be some blood thirsty bandits eager to slit his throat.

But that was the chance he had to take; the dreams of Robbie persisted. It was almost as though he could see where he was and that he was crying out to be rescued. As a rational man, he did not believe in "second sight" but something besides his rational mind was pulling him deeper and deeper into this desert.

When Brahim awoke he looked about him sleepily, as if he had forgotten where he was and why he had come. Then he narrowed his eyes and looked at Rick. "Best we stop soon, or go back. We will never find them if they don't contact us. To stay out here alone another night is too dangerous. My captain, he didn't tell me to get killed, only to keep you out of trouble if I could."

Rick stopped the Jeep and looked at him calmly. "Then you are welcome to walk back," he said bitterly. "I haven't come all this far just to turn back. I've come to make contact with my son's kidnapers and if this is where we have to spend the night to do it, then here is where I will stay. But as I said before, you are welcome to walk back."

Brahim looked at him morosely, then pulled the hood of his geleba over his face, crossed his arms and sank into angry silence. Rick drove grimly. Several times the motor coughed as though it were about to give out, but then it restarted with a vengeance. Rick felt as though his own anger and desperation were driving it, as if he were willing it to go forward.

By dusk they were in the foothills of the blue mountains. The sky had been getting steadily darker and the wind blowing more and more gustily. Light showers of sand began to infiltrate the jeep. Rick could taste it on his lips, gritty and hard. Brahim touched his shoulder, his anger seemingly dissipated in a larger fear. "Best we stop and take shelter. *Gibli* is coming. No one will find us then."

The wind grew fiercer. Bringing with it clouds of rust colored sand that covered the windshield like solid rain.

Unable to move forward any more, or see where he was going. Rick stopped the Jeep and, grabbing a can of water and some blankets from the rack above the Jeep. He then ordered Brahim into the back seat. "Close up every crack that you can and cover your face," he told the frightened policeman. "We'll just have to sit this one out." The sky was as dark as night now and the wind was howling so loudly that it was impossible to hear even his own voice. But he still seemed to hear Robbie's voice crying for help on the wind.

It was almost daybreak when he awoke from his cramped position in the front seat. He was greeted by a silence so profound that for a moment he thought that he had lost his hearing. The Jeep was totally dark, and as he lit his pocket flashlight, he could see that the sand not only covered the windshield, but had penetrated the cabin and covered his legs and feet. He struggled to free himself and with care, stuck his arm out the top of the window to see if he could free it from the sand. Finally his fingers wiggled free into air above him. He worked frantically to clear a passage for air and when this was done, fell again into a fitful sleep.

He was awakened next by Brahim's moaning. Somehow the Arab boy had cut his head and he was mopping at the blood and mumbling prayers to Allah at the same time. Rick told him to be quiet. Brahim continued to moan and mumble prayers. A harsh voice from outside speaking in guttural Arabic silenced him, accompanied by the sound of digging.

"We should leave them to die," said one angry voice.

"Yes, but let us first find if they have food or money," said another. "Then we can kill them."

Brahim's prayers became louder and louder, until a poke from Rick silenced him. "Save your breath to reason with these bastards," he whispered. "We may have found what we were looking for."

Brahim rolled his eyes heavenward. But he stopped praying out loud.

The windshield was partially cleared now. And in the early light of dawn Rick got a look at their rescuers. They were young men wearing ragged desert clothing. One of them was missing several front teeth. The other had a missing hand. Brahim, sucked in his breath at the sight of the missing hand. "That is a bad one," he said. "Do not tell him that I am with the police. It will not go well with us."

Rick touched the pistol at his belt and loaded his inside pockets with several more rounds of ammunition. The door to the Jeep was almost clear now and Rick spoke to Brahim in a whisper. "Tell them that I am a photo journalist and that we are doing a story on the Algerian revolution. We want to tell their story to the world. See how that goes down with them."

Brahim began babbling almost before the door was opened. Thanking the men for saving them and asking the blessings of Allah upon them for their noble deed. His approach clearly took the men aback for a few moments. Then they hauled him roughly from the back seat and began to question him. Rick noticed, to his relief, that they seemed unarmed except for a rude sort of club that the man with only one hand carried. They glanced in Rick's direction several times as Brahim continued his story. Finally, shaking their fists, they demanded that Rick get out of the Jeep.

He emerged slowly, his right hand held casually over his pistol. As he stood up, the sand poured out of his clothes moving across his skin like silk. He could still taste it in his mouth, and he longed for a drink of water. But he stood tall, towering over the two young men, and greeted them in Arabic as though this were a social encounter.

They looked curiously at his clothes and peered into the Jeep hungrily. Then the one with the club spoke menacingly again and shook his good arm at Brahim, who answered smoothly, gesturing at the water can. They smelled it first and then drank deeply. Rick could feel his own throat contract with a need to swallow. But he stifled it, continuing to stand casually by the side of the Jeep, with his hand at his belt covering his side-arm.

Then Brahim offered them some dried meat. They eyed it hungrily. After a minutes hesitation they grabbed it, still eyeing Rick and his armed stance, they ate like animals, chewing and slobbering. Brahim watched them in disgust, his fear now dissipated. His only desire now was to get back to town and to a clean uniform and away from these desert barbarians. Rick, however, had other ideas.

Once the men had eaten he began to ask them questions through Brahim. Had they heard of anyone keeping a blonde boy captive in this part of the desert? Had there been rumors? Had they seen or heard anything?

The men looked at one another, then shrugged and continued eating. Then the one with teeth missing rubbed his two fingers together in the universal sign for money, as he grabbed another piece of the dried meat. Brahim shook his head in disgust, and answered them angrily. Clearly he felt that giving these men money would be a waste of time.

Rick shrugged and pointed at his pockets, indicating that they were empty. But he took several cans of food out of the jeep and placed them tantalizing on the sand in front of the men. They gazed at them hungrily, looking at one another.

Rick took out two more cans of a sweet sugary drink and added them to the pile. The men moved toward them but Rick put his hand to his belt and eyed them sternly. "Brahim, tell them no more food unless they give us information. I want the truth, even if they know nothing."

The men eyed one another and then the tantalizing cans of food and drink which were seldom seen in the desert. One of them began to speak in guttural Arabic, glancing at his companion from time to time, to see if he was going too far.

Brahim, returning to his policeman demeanor, held up his hand for silence while he translated for Rick. "They say that they have heard of a blonde boy who is the prisoner of one of the desert chieftains. He holds him hoping for money to continue his war against the government in Algiers. This man is very dangerous they say. He will cut off your head if you look at him the wrong way. They have already been punished by him. They hate him but they are also very afraid of him. He kills without mercy. Sometimes even his own men."

The two Arabs nodded and made cutting motions with their hands, all the while eyeing the food on the sand in front of them.

"And where can this chief be found?" Rick asked through Brahim. The men pointed behind them, toward the mountains, shrugging their shoulders and opening their arms wide.

"They say that he can be anywhere. He is like the wind. He has a small band and they travel fast. They do not take prisoners and they leave their enemies to die in the desert like dogs." Brahim translated slowly, looking less and less enthusiastic about the mission his chief had sent him on.

"Then we will find them," Rick answered. Pushing the food toward the two hungry men. "When they have finished eating, tell them that we wish to be led to the last place they saw this man. We will give them food and pay them. But I must find the boy."

The men grinned evilly hearing this news, and again consulted with each other in their guttural language, which Brahim reluctantly translated. "They do not want to go near this place again. They are afraid that they will be killed and that we will too. But they will show us part of the way for food and money."

Rick made a rapid calculation. There was enough food and water for two men for three more days. Having the extra two men to feed would be an unnecessary strain on their resources. It also gave them one more person to keep an eye on. He told Brahim to bargain to leave one man behind and to take one with them in the Jeep. This way the journey would be faster and there would be one less mouth to feed. After a long harangue, this was agreed upon. The one-handed man would stay behind and continue back to his village. The snaggle-toothed one would lead them to the spot where the chieftain had last been seen.

Rick knew that he was clutching at straws, hoping for a miracle, for some evidence that Robbie was still alive. That somewhere in this vast wasteland a freckled faced boy was waiting and hoping that his father would come for him. He could not ignore that call. He would risk his worthless life for it, and do it alone if necessary.

*   *   *

Janine was in her motel room regrouping after the luncheon with Jean Claude. She felt sticky and in need of a swim but she turned on the overhead fan and tried again to reach the Embassy secure line. This time the security officer answered and she reported on her position and her dilemma.

"Keep your eye on Bonet," was the reply. "We are more and more sure that he holds the key to the puzzle. He is not a man who makes pleasure trips. If he is in D'Jerba, there must be a reason. Find out what it is. And don't be out of touch so long."

Janine ground her teeth as she hung up. "Don't be out of touch for so long," indeed. In other words, "Call us when you've figured it all out, and don't ask for us until then."

The agency was run by a bunch of macho guys, and they really resented women operatives unless it was for playing house. Well, to hell with them. She would figure this out herself and rub their noses in it before she was finished.

She put on a swim suit and threw a towel over her shoulders. The beach looked deserted and so did the pool. But she decided on the beach so she could avoid the others. She still needed time to think. Von Grantz and his side-kick had been conspicuous by their absence. They were usually snooping around muttering to each other in German. Their absence left a strange void. She hadn't seen them since yesterday and that was unusual.

As if she had conjured them up, they appeared at the far end of the beach, fully dressed and deep in conversation. They looked as though they had been on some kind of expedition. They both wore desert boots and Hanz, the aide-de-camp, carried a small shovel. They looked for a way to avoid meeting her, but seeing none, they advanced toward her, shoulders stiff, eyes cold.

They would have passed her without speaking. But Janine wouldn't allow it. Since she had more of less been told to figure this all out by herself some imp of Satan possessed her. "Been taking up archaeology," she said breezily as they passed her. "I think that the French have already dug up all the good stuff around here."

Von Grantz stiffened. His face turned a dark beet red at his effort not to strike her. Hanz gulped and tried unsuccessfully to hide the shovel behind his back. Then they bowed stiffly almost in unison and mumbled a greeting in German. "We are collecting shells for our wives," von Grantz added. "So interesting the sea life in this area, don't you think?"

"So is the low life," Janine said, smiling sweetly as she swung her towel over her shoulder and proceeded down the beach looking for a place to take a dip.

Von Grantz watched her, his eyes narrowed. "This woman is not amusing, and she is not what she seems to be. I would like to get permission to get rid of her permanently."

"That will not be easy, *Mein Herr*. Bonet seems to enjoy her company."

"Then he is a fool and we are fools to be working for him. If the shipment continues to be delayed, we will all be at risk. I do not like this Tunisian Ahmed. I think that he has been sent to spy on us and that is why the chemicals have not arrived. He spends his time sniffing after the American woman. Why?"

"She is very beautiful, *Mein Herr*, perhaps that is why."

"Don't show your stupidity, she is the daughter of a great American Industrialist. That is why. He wants information from her."

Hanz giggled. "He also wants something else. And he seems to be getting it."

Just then Melanie passed them with Ahmed in tow. She wore a tiny bikini under a huge beach towel which was wrapped around her like a sarong. Ahmed wore a terry cloth robe and gave the Germans a smoldering look as he passed.

They muttered a greeting and then went back to their whispered conversation in German.

"Only we know where the triggering device is hidden. That is our life insurance policy with Bonet. He needs to trade that to get safe passage of the chemicals. As long as only we know where it is we are safe," von Grantz hissed in his sibilant German.

"*Ja*," answered Hanz, looking around nervously. "But if he wants to find out, he has ways that are not pleasant."

"Be assured that if you are tempted to talk, I will kill you first. I intend to go back to Germany as a rich man. Neither your stupidity or Bonet's games will deter me from that goal."

"Not his games, but perhaps his bullets," said Hanz morosely, dragging his feet in the soft sand as they walked back to their room. "I would be much happier if all this were over and we were drinking a good glass of schnapps in Berlin."

"Think of drinking later. Now we need to plan what we are going to tell Bonet when he calls." He stopped and looked out into the empty bay. "He will be very angry that nothing is going as planned. The Tunisian officer is behind the delay, I'm sure. If the military find out what Bonet is up to, it will be the end of his commercial schemes. They are very afraid of repeating what has happened in Algeria here." He slapped Hanz on the back in a calculated gesture of intimacy, as the two moved down the beach.

Janine watched them go. From their hunched shoulders and secretive attitude she could tell that they were up to something, but what. To bad that she didn't have a bugging device planted on one of them. It might be worth while putting one in their room. The Germans had certainly been scarce since Bonet arrived. Almost as if they were avoiding any contact with him or showing any interest in what he was doing. It was too unlike their ordinary behavior to be true.

The group all dined together that evening in the patio of the hotel. The sun was just turning into an orb of golden fire behind the fig trees and date palms. There was a slight breeze, and for a moment Janine could believe that she was really on a diplomatic boondoggle, babysitting a couple of innocent German scientists, instead of risking her neck in a dangerous game which was becoming daily more unclear.

Ahmed seemed thoroughly enthralled with Melanie, feeding her tidbits of cous cous from his plate and laughing as she licked it off her prominent lower lip. The Germans watched them in stony silence, any pretense of politeness gone. Brian had retreated also into his Virginia gentleman mode, saying little but keeping his eyes fixed on Janine for clues to her reactions.

The German's tension during the meal was almost palpable. They worked their way through three courses of spicy Tunisian food with almost no reaction. By the time the sugary desert was served, Janine was sure that they were up to something. Von Grantz suddenly began to talk to Ahmed, while Hanz made an awkward attempt to engage Melanie in conversation. Melanie ignored him as though he were some lower life form, at the same time clinging to Ahmed's arm. But finally, something that von Grantz said seemed to get Ahmed's attention. He listened quietly for a few minutes and then glanced down at his watch and then nodded as though agreeing.

Janine's stomach gave a tell-tale lurch. The Germans were clearly up to something, and whatever it was didn't bode well for Ahmed or herself. She saw Brian's across the table watching her, she nodded at him and then excused herself, saying that she didn't want any of the strong Arab coffee. "It's the only thing in the world that keeps me from sleeping," she lied. "And tonight I plan to turn in early," she lied again.

She went back to her room and after splashing in the bathroom a bit she put on black jeans and a black long sleeved shirt and tucked her pistol with a silencer on it into the holster under her arm. Then she darkened the room so that she could open the blinds enough to see outside. The sky was bright with just a sliver of a moon, enough to light up the courtyard and to illuminate the space between the dining room and the rest of the stucco cottages. She saw von Grantz return to his room and emerge almost immediately carrying something at his side, like a rifle in a case. Hanz came out of the dining room next, followed by Melanie and Ahmed. It looked as though Melanie was trying to entice Ahmed into a moonlight walk, but when he resisted, she shrugged her shoulders and walked down the beach with the long suffering Brian.

"I'm going to personally see that boy gets a promotion." Janine promised herself, as she slid out the door to follow von Grantz down the beach in the opposite direction. He was walking quickly, his head bent low and his shoulders hunched, as though he were trying to make himself smaller. The rifle at his side looked like a third leg. His partner was no-where to be seen.

Finally von Grantz stopped near a large outcropping of rock. The sea was breaking at the foot of it and von Grantz had to wade into the water to get a footing to climb higher up the rock, bracing himself on the rifle stock as though it were a cane. Janine hugged the land side of the rock, just out of his line of vision. Three palm trees leaned into the wind at the water line. Perhaps this was the landmark that von Grantz had given Ahmed. But he was going to get more than an information exchange, if that was what von Grantz had promised him. A bullet in the gut was probably more like it. The German must be desperate to use such an obvious ambush. Janine couldn't believe that Ahmed would fall for it.

But there he was, walking casually down the beach as though out for an evening stroll. Hanz followed a few paces behind him, muttering in German. "This is the place *Mein Herr* indicated. We were to wait for him here." Ahmed uttered an Arabic oath desecrating the German's parentage, which fortunately the German didn't understand. Janine heard a faint sound above her. Von Grantz must have scaled the cliff an be on the other side but with a clear view of the beach. A few pebbles rolled down, one striking her on the cheek confirming his hiding place.

She saw the flare of a match and in the light could see Ahmed's face as he lit a cigarette. He didn't seem to be armed, and the glow from the tip of his cigarette made him a perfect target, should von Grantz decide to ambush him now. Another shower of falling rock told her that von Grantz was getting into position. She pulled the pistol from its holster and removed the silencer, then fired into the air over her head to warn Ahmed. She heard a scream and a oath in German and then silence. Ahmed pushed Hanz into the sand and looked in the direction of the scream.

Janine, still hidden by the rocks, replaced her gun and backed into the shadows. Whatever Ahmed found on the cliff above he would have to deal with himself. At least he had been warned in time.

She hugged the shadows on the way back to her cabana. Her shirt was wet with perspiration and her mouth was dry. There were entirely too many games being played on this mission, and most of them didn't make any sense at all. Why was von Grantz suddenly after Ahmed? He was taking a great chance attacking a Tunisian military officer. And if he had really meant to kill him, it would even be worse. What had forced him to take such desperate measures? It didn't make any sense at all.

To all appearances von Grantz was just what he pretended to be, a chemical engineer, not an assassin. The attempt was so clumsy that Ahmed would probably not have been hurt at all, unless von Grantz had gotten him on the first shot from his hiding place on the cliff. She reached her cabana in the dark and let herself into a quiet room. She had just finished peeling off her dark clothes and putting on a dressing gown when she heard voices outside.

She opened the door cautiously, to see Hanz carrying the limp body of von Grantz into the compound. The body was very still and Hanz was sobbing openly. Ahmed was nowhere to be seen. Janine opened her door quietly and went out into the patio. She was quickly joined by Melanie and Brian and the hotel owner who began to wring his hands and wail in Arabic. At Janine's insistence, Hanz deposited the body on a lounge chair next to the pool. Von Grantz's head rolled limply and there was a large bleeding wound on his forehead, which looked like a bullet had entered at close range. There was no pulse and the body was already getting cold. There was also no sign of the rifle.

"What happened to him Hanz," Janine asked, in her best professional manner, with her heart beating ridiculously hard. This brought forth another sobbing tirade from Hanz which even Janine found hard to interpret. He had gone for a walk with Herr Ahmed to meet Herr von Grantz after dinner. There had been a shot and a scream and then Herr Ahmed had found Herr von Grantz on the cliff above the beach, shot in the head and his neck broken.

Janine examined the wound again. It might well have been from her gun. But the broken neck was someone else's doing. She immediately thought of Ahmed, who was certainly canny enough to know that he was being set up, and would have had no compunctions about finishing the job that she had accidentally started. But where was the rifle? If the police were to find that, it would certainly start an inquiry. Civilians were forbidden to carry guns. Perhaps that's where Ahmed was now, taking care of the evidence, and probably the police too, if she knew the military.

At that moment Ahmed appeared out of the shadows, shaking his head. "Whoever the assassins were, they are gone now. And they covered their tracks very well." He touched von Grantz's neck at the main artery. Then he looked directly at Janine. "I guess that Hanz and I were lucky to get away alive. They may have been gunning for all of us. I suggest that we all stay inside our rooms until the police arrive, especially the women."

Chapter Thirteen

Janine spent the half hour before the police arrived carefully taking apart her weapon and hiding it in various places in her room. The Tunisian police were well known for their attitude about civilians carrying guns. And even though she had diplomatic immunity, she didn't want to risk being declared *persona non grata* and being shipped out of the country right now.

The Germans were up to something very unsavory and she had a strong feeling that Bonet was behind it. He would have had no compunction about getting rid of Ahmed, or of using von Grantz to do it. But why had he employed such an amateur assassin, and such a public beach?

Either he was overconfident or in too much of a hurry to plan carefully. But whatever he was doing, the stakes must be high to risk striking at a Tunisian military officer. Especially one with friends in high places like Ahmed.

She finished hiding the dismantled pistol, and dressed carefully in her lady diplomat clothes. She tried calling the Embassy to warn the Ambassador about what had happened, but as usual, got his answering machine.

Then on a wild chance that she might get him, she tried Sam at home in Washington. This was one time when she needed some backup. Besides, he had started them all off on this merry-go-round. Sam answered after a number of rings. She could almost smell his late afternoon drink in his gravely voice. His first question was, "Is this line secure."

"Let's hope so," Janine answered, telling him quickly what had happened, using general code words that he would understand, but which would be hard for the Tunisians to translate. When she finished, there was a moment's silence, then Sam's clipped tones.

"I take it you're on your own with this? You've made no mention of your partner."

"He's out treasure hunting in the desert," Janine answered dryly. "No help at all"

"And the Big Kahuna?", Sam asked, using the Ambassador's code name.

"Essentially told me to use my own initiative and not to bother him with details," Janine replied.

"Well my advice to you is to check your 'bonnet' very carefully. But be careful, the wind down there can get very strong. We even feel it here in Washington. But most people here think that you won't have a lot of time to enjoy your vacation in D'Jerba before it gets much too hot down there."

"In other words, come home?" Janine asked hopefully.

Sam sighed. "Wish I could invite you, but at the moment you have to keep an eye on the 'bonnet' you have, until you can get a new one in Paris. But stay in touch and I'll see what I can do."

Janine clicked off the cellular, just as there was a knock on her door. She took a careful look around and put the phone in her briefcase and locked it, before she opened the door.

Ahmed stood there, with a tired looking Tunisian police officer. He was obviously impressed with the gravity of his mission, but a bit in awe of the Ahmed, who took the lead in the questioning. He carefully wrote down Janine's answers in a small notebook. She remained calm and professional and didn't volunteer any information.

She was amazed at Ahmed's savoir-faire. He was leading the police to the conclusion that it had been some kind of accident. A fall from a cliff, a broken neck, so sad. No mention was made of the bullet hole in the middle of von Grantz's forehead. That clearly would be bad for tourism, and was better forgotten.

After a routine chat with the others in the compound, the policeman directed that the body, wrapped in a sheet and elongated on a stretcher, be driven away in a police van.

Hanz was beside himself with anger. Shaking his fist after the departing van. "*Mein Herr* is killed, and they do nothing. It was not an accident. I myself heard the shot." Then he began to sob brokenly.

Janine took him by the arm and led him towards her cabana. "Let me offer you some brandy, Hanz", she said, in what she hoped passed for her most motherly tones. "You have had a terrible shock. Come and sit for a moment, and let me get you something to drink."

He followed her blindly, like a small, chubby child moaning over a lost pet. When she had him seated in the armchair in her room, she poured him a stiff shot of brandy in a tooth brush glass. He drank it down almost immediately and she replenished it several times while sipping modestly on her own.

"He was such a good engineer, Herr von Grantz. Ve vere going to do vonderful things," he said, holding out his glass for more brandy." He vas verry, verry smart," he said tapping himself on the temple. Not like me. Now I don't know vat to do…" His voice trailed off and he looked piteously at Janine. "How do I know that they don't kill me next. Dat is vat I am afraid of."

Janine seized her chance. "Why should anyone want to kill you?", she said soothingly." What have you done?"

Hanz looked at her accusingly. "I have done nothing," he mumbled, "only followed orders to help Herr von Grantz and now he is dead. Now they will kill me too, because of the *machina*."

"What '*machina*', "Janine asked softly, soothing him with the use of his mother tongue, while pouring him another brandy.

Hanz looked at her with bleary eyes half filled with tears. "The one he made us hide in the caves, to trade for money. It is a very important '*machina*', "he said, just before his head rolled forward and he emitted a loud snore.

Janine waited a moment, and then shook him gently by the shoulder. "Do you know where the '*machina*' is Hanz?" she asked in German. "Can you take me to it?"

He opened his eyes sleepily, barely focusing on her. "*Ya, ya, ya shatze,*" he said dreamily. "*Ich kan du mitnamen.*" He put a drunken finger to his fat lips. "Don't tell the *Fuhrer.*" Then he giggled. "Herr Bonet will be very angry if I tell."

Janine sat in the darkened room for awhile listening to Hanz snore. The noise of his sleeping drowned anything from outside the room and she was grateful for a few moments to reflect on what to do next.

Clearly von Grantz and Hanz had hidden something in the caves on the other side of the island, something that they had hoped to sell or trade in a deal which Bonet may not have known about. Or found out about too late to stop them. It may have been a clumsy attempt to line their own pockets at the expense of whatever Bonet was up to in D'Jerba, or it may have been part of Bonet's plan. But it looked as though Hanz was now an important part of the puzzle. Keeping an eye on him and keeping him alive was going to be her main job for the next few days. It was not one that she was looking forward to.

She walked outside to find Ahmed waiting for her in the shadows outside her room. "Find out anything?" he asked, his eyes glowing black in the light of his cigarette.

"Only that he is a sad little man, missing his colleague," Janine answered, stalling for time.

Ahmed's jaw hardened. "I think that it is time that you and I stopped playing games," he said, pulling her around so that she faced him squarely. "I know that you shot Grantz. I don't care why. As far as I am concerned, he was vermin, but he is an important link to the evidence we need to keep him and his kind out of Tunisia. I need to know what you found out, and I need to know it right away."

He pulled her to him roughly. "We both want the same thing—to stop this madness. If they had their way, the whole Arab world would be fighting each other and killing each other off with the weapons they provide in exchange for our oil. They care for nothing, only money. So tell me what you know. Both of our countries will profit by your honesty."

Janine winced in pain. He seemed perfectly capable of tearing off her arm if she didn't respond. And for all she knew, they might be on the same side. "If you stop twisting my arm, I'll tell you," she gasped.

He released his grip slightly, but continued to hold her close, so that anyone passing would think that they were having a lover's tete-a-tete. Janine thought quickly about how much to reveal. The agency dealt harshly with those who made mistakes about whom to place their confidence in.

But at the moment Ahmed was the only game in town. There wasn't much that she could do alone, especially with him dogging her footsteps, and Bonet's men not far behind. She decided to risk a partial truth.

"I only know that he and von Grantz have hidden something somewhere along this coast. I don't know what it is or where it is. Only that they planned to sell it or trade it to someone who is coming for it soon. They expected to realize a lot of money from it's sale," she said, rubbing her arm, as Ahmed released his grip slightly. "Hanz knows where it is, but I don't know what it will take to get him to lead me to it."

"And what part does the Frenchman Bonet play in this?" Ahmed asked, rubbing the back of his hand along her cheek.

Janine recoiled, but then held her ground. It would not do to let the Arab know that she was afraid of him, at least of his superior size and strength. "I'm not sure," Janine lied. "He is part of a very large and influential international company. He would be risking the company's position and his own place in it if he were involved in something illegal."

Ahmed smiled bitterly. "You and I both know what men are tempted to do for money. It is the same in France as in America, or in my country. Men do what they must to survive." He rubbed his chin thoughtfully.

"Join me at first light on the beach, and bring the German with you. Perhaps together we can persuade him to tell us what he knows." As Janine opened the door to her cabana, he added in an undertone. "Whatever you do, don't let him out of your room tonight."

Janine opened the door softly. The German was still in her chair snoring softly. With Ahmed's help she tied his legs to the chair, so if he tried to get up he would awaken her. Then she lay on top of her bed, fully clothed and tried to sleep.

Her arm still ached where Ahmed had held it and her brain kept running through various scenarios. Bonet and von Grantz, von Grantz and Hanz, Duke Weston far away in New York, perhaps pulling the strings to make all this happen. Rick in the desert looking for Weston's grandson. Melanie in D'Jerba. There must be a pattern to all this, but what was it? What were they after? She spent some of this time silently retrieving and reassembling her gun and then lay down on the bed with it beside her.

She woke with a start. There was light coming through the curtains, and Hanz was frantically trying to free himself from the armchair. He seemed in pain, until Janine remembered how much of the brandy he had drunk the night before. She watched him struggle for a moment, then told him that she would let him go in one condition, that he show her where he and von Grantz had hidden the *machina*.

At first he shook his head stubbornly, then as his need grew greater, he agreed, trembling as he told her. Janine opened the bathroom door with the barrel of her gun, and kept it on his back as he relieved himself. Then she tied him in the chair again and waited for Ahmed to arrive.

* * *

Rick awoke before dawn. The first light was creeping up on the blue mountains, outlining them in a circle of gold. Near him two sleeping bodies, wrapped in woolen gelabas, snored peacefully. They were almost at the foot of the mountains now, looking up. There was no sign of life or of any human habitation. The snaggle toothed Arab had told him that this is where he had last seen the bandits and Robbie.

Rick had less and less confidence in his story. They had seen nothing, no sign of humans or even of horses. Brahim was constantly urging that they turn back. Nothing would be served, he argued, by their dying here in the desert of being killed by Algerian rebels.

"They cut off your head like a melon, just for sport." He argued, his eyes growing round and frightened. The snaggle toothed one agreed, but then he shook his head soberly and agreed with anything that Brahim said.

Rick stretched and relieved himself. Then he drank a sip of their precious water, dreaming of hot black coffee. He checked his gun and his ammunition. There was enough to defend themselves for awhile, but not to hold out against a group of armed bandits.

He must be out of his mind to be trying this alone with two frightened Arabs. If he had any sense, he would be frightened too. The stories coming out of Algeria about atrocities against foreigners had been more than graphic recently, slaughter without reason and without cause, seemingly done only for the pleasure of drawing blood. He shuddered. If Robbie had fallen into rebel hands, was there any reason for them to keep him alive?

He touched Brahim's sleeping form with his foot, arousing him from slumber. They needed time to talk while the snaggle toothed one slept. There was just enough gas to get back to the border town; they couldn't risk using the Jeep much longer. Any travel today would have to be on foot and it would take them straight ahead, up the mountain.

Brahim agreed and volunteered to stay with the Jeep while Rick and the snaggle toothed one explored the mountain. Rick smiled grimly. It was almost as if he could read the policeman's thoughts.

"Thanks," he said, dismantling the distributor and pocketing the keys. "If I'm not back by sundown, come after me with more ammunition."

Snaggle tooth led him reluctantly up a barely visible mountain trail, helped by an occasional nudge from the butt of Rick's gun. When they were half way up, Rick shared a bit of jerky with him for encouragement. He could see Brahim and the Jeep far below, looking like a child's Christmas toy. He suddenly felt a lump in his throat. How long ago it had been since he and Robbie had shared a Christmas. Perhaps they never would again.

He got to his feet and grimly urged snaggle tooth to do the same. The Arab pointed to dried horse droppings at the side of the path and shook his head in terror, pointing up the path and shaking his head. Then throwing himself to his knees and prostrating himself in what he believed was the direction of Mecca.

Rick looked with disgust at his prostrate form, then dismissed him with the toe of his boot. He would make better time without him and the man had fulfilled his promise, more or less. Better to do this alone now. There was less chance of being discovered and he could certainly travel faster up the mountain by himself.

The man scuttled sideways, like a crab, when released, then down the path without looking back, except to prostrate himself one more time, clearly believing that Allah was responsible for his early release. "There goes another believer," Rick muttered to himself as he hiked rapidly up the mountain path.

It grew cooler as he got higher. There were rocky outcroppings on both sides of the path. The bandits had chosen their location well. It would be hard for anyone to follow them up here and not be seen and there were plenty of hiding places along the way.

Rick stopped for a few moments in the shadow of one of the large rocks. Far down below he could see the snaggle toothed one still scurrying down the rocks. Then suddenly there was the sound of a shot and the man tumbled head first down the rest of the path, rolling head over heels like a broken doll. Rick retreated further into the shadow of the rock.

Brahim was too far below to have heard the shot, or at least he made no reaction to it. There was no cover on the path down, and precious little on the way up. But Rick continued to climb, staying off the path and in the shadow of the rocks. He could see a rocky outcropping above him, which would make a perfect look out spot. But searching it with his field glasses, he couldn't make out anyone there. But the shot hadn't been random. It was well aimed and deadly.

As he climbed higher, he began to hear shouts, then a sound, like women wailing. It intensified as he climbed parallel to the path, but far to the right of it. Then he heard shots, receding in the distance and shouts and women's cries.

Soon he was looking down on the flat outlook rock. It sheltered a camp of some kind, which looked as if it had just been hastily evacuated. There were slaughtered men and animals all around the camp and a few women wandering aimlessly around making a high pitched wail. They were throwing dust into the air over their heads, emitting a shrill sound of mourning.

Rick watched them for a few minutes. Was this a trap? But their grief seemed real.

One tall, slender woman separated herself from the group and began to wander in circles taking short steps like a Geisha. She wore a ragged filthy dress and her head was covered with a dirty scarf. She wandered in the direction of the ledge, walked out on it and stood looking down, as if trying to decide whether or not to jump and end her misery. There was something about her that was troublingly familiar to Rick.

He eased his way along the ledge, swearing as his foot dislodged a shower of stones. The woman looked up startled. Even from a distance Rick thought that he recognized the "woman" as Robbie. Astonished, he crept toward him across the rocks, keeping his head down and his hand on his pistol.

Robbie gave no sign of recognition. He swayed back and forth on the ledge, as though he were about to fall or jump. For one agonizing moment, it looked as if he had decided to end his life. Rick got to him just in time to grab him around the legs and pull him back from the edge as he was about to let himself fall over it.

They tussled for a moment, but the boy was thin and exhausted and no match for his father's strength. But he fought with all the strength he had, until he collapsed in weeping exhaustion.

Rick pinned him to the ledge, putting a hand over his mouth to keep him from crying out. The boy showed no sign of recognition. His blue eyes were clouded and his body gave off a terrible stench. Rick gagged at the smell.

Then the boy suddenly went limp, as though the struggle had exhausted his last ounce of strength. His head rolled to the side and Rick could see burn marks and bruises on his neck. He held the boy to him for a moment, despite the stench, and swore an oath of revenge on whoever had done this to his son.

The women were now busy skinning the dead animals and seeing to the wounded and paid no attention to what was happening on the ledge. There were still occasional gun shots in the distance, as though all the able bodied men were still after the marauders.

Rick eased Robbie over his shoulder and began the steep decent, stopping every few yards to adjust his burden. The boy showed no sign of life, but Rick could feel his shallow breathing against his shoulder as he half ran, half slid down the mountain.

Finally, he came to a resting place near where snaggle tooth's body was lying. He lay Robbie down on the ground. The boy's eyes were open now and he stared a Rick with no sign of recognition.

His wrists had deep bleeding scars, as though his hands had been tied for some time, and his legs were still hobbled, which explained his mincing walk. Rick cut the hobble and tried to get the boy to stand on his feet. He obeyed and then fell to his knees weeping, seemingly too weak to move.

Rick got him to his feet again and half dragged, half pulled him down the mountain. Whatever was happening on the mountaintop wasn't going to last too long. He needed to get back to the Jeep and to extra ammunition and any backup that Brahim could offer.

Robbie stumbled and Rick reached out a hand to help him, but the boy pulled back in terror, mumbling something in Arabic. But he did seem to understand that he was escaping and began to hurry down the mountain, slipping and sliding.

There was a noise up above them now and rifle shots began to ricochet off the rocks above them. They kept low and hugged the rocks until they were almost out of range and in sight of the Jeep.

They ran the last few yards with Brahim covering them with his weapon. Rick bundled Robbie into the back seat and cursing his previous precaution with the distributor, hastily replaced the missing parts.

The Jeep started with a sputter and a cough. There was intermittent rifle fire from above, but it no longer seemed to be coming in their direction.

"They will kill each other, good," the boy said in Arabic, and then he again fell silent.

"Who is this woman?", Brahim asked. "Why have you brought her with us, she stinks like a pig."

"She may lead me to my son." Rick said softly, hoping to hide Robbie's shame a little longer, while he decided how to bring him back to life and to get him into Tunisia without any one finding out about him, until he was again in his right mind.

Rick floored the accelerator, hoping that the bandits would keep each other occupied for a little while longer. At least long enough to put a comfortable distance between them. No more shots were fired, but the boy in the back seat kept up a crooning noise that was at best unnerving.

"What will you do with this woman?" Brahim asked almost in anger. "She sounds crazy to me and we can't take an Algerian woman with us back into Tunisia. Believe me, there are plenty of women in my country who smell a lot better than this, and who are a whole lot prettier."

Rick grunted an answer. "She is important to my mission, and that should be enough for you."

"Then she must be the wife of the chief, why else would you bother with her. But let's make her bathe before we give her back."

"We aren't giving her back," Rick said grimly. "We are taking her with us one way or another. I want you to start thinking about how we are going to get her across the border."

Brahim looked over at him in amazement. But seeing Rick's expression, he knew him to be in earnest. He sighed, then rubbed his head with his hand.

"Then we must go south by Touzeur, but we must find a *hamam* and wash her somewhere on the way. No one will receive us with such a dirty woman," he said in distress.

"Then we will wash ourselves as well," Rick said. "We probably don't smell very good either, after three days in the desert."

"*Ensh 'alla*," said Brahim. "If it is the will of Allah," and fell into a brooding silence that was unlike his usually cheerful disposition.

Rick turned the Jeep away from the mountains and set out across the desert, hoping that their gas supply would hold out until they got to the next oasis which was rudely etched on the map he carried.

They reached the oasis just before nightfall. It was on the edge of a salt plateau that reached into the desert. A few scraggly palm trees and some mud huts marked its outlines.

The villagers were openly suspicious of them, going into their houses and slamming the doors. One elderly man barred the door of his house and stood in front of it with a wooden club. He shouted at them in Arabic and shook his fist, looking as frightening as an angry old turkey gobbler.

"They are afraid of us, sir," said Brahim, translating. "They say that the bandits have already taken everything, all their food and have slaughtered their animals and stolen their women. He asks if we come to do worse."

"Tell him that we come in peace. "We only want to wash ourselves and our sick friend and rest for the night. We will leave them unharmed," Rick said, fingering his gun. "Tell them we only wish a little water to wash, and then we will be on our way tomorrow."

The man looked at them suspiciously, then held out his hand in the universal gesture for money. Rick gave him some coins, which seemed to satisfy him, and then he led the way to a well and a rough bath house at the edge of the small oasis.

The air was immediately cooler here and the scraggly date palms cast some shadow over the pool. The man indicated the place for bathing and then backed away as if not wanting to watch them pollute his pool with their foreign bodies.

Robbie had followed them in silence, his head held low and his stinking women's garments clutched about him. Rick knew that this was the moment of truth. He would have to strip him to wash him and then it would be immediately evident that he wasn't really a girl.

Brahim's reaction was immediate and predictable. He looked horrified as Rick began to strip off the woman's clothes. And even more so when Robbie's naked body revealed that he wasn't a woman at all, but a light skinned, freckled boy covered with cuts and bruises.

Brahim looked at him curiously. "They have used this boy as a woman," he said, spitting on the ground to show his contempt. "This is not an honorable thing to do if the boy is unwilling, and young and a foreigner."

Rick nodded, too angry to respond. But he washed Robbie gently. The boy shivered and winced when the water touched his cuts. He seemed lost in a world of his own. A world that he had retreated into to save himself from the horror of the last few weeks.

He looked at Rick without recognition, but he allowed himself to be washed and dressed in some of Rick's outsized clothes and then settled on the bank of the pool. While the two men hastily washed themselves, he stared into space unmoving.

The water felt slightly warm and gritty to Rick's tired body. But it was wet and somewhat clean, despite the odd smell. Rick washed his hair and new beard, and watched as Brahim did the same, all the time looking curiously at the boy on the bank.

"How did you know that it was not a woman, sir," he asked Rick cautiously. "And who is this boy that we have rescued from the bandits?"

"He was my son," Rick answered wearily. "And perhaps he will be again. At the moment he doesn't seem to know who he is. That is why I must get him back into Tunisia and to some medical help as soon as possible. Can you help me get him across the border without papers?"

Brahim looked dubious. "That is a difficult thing that you ask. Now that he is clean, it is clear that he is not Arab. The Algerians will not let him leave unless we tell a very good story and give them a lot of money, and even then it is not sure. They could take the money and then shoot us," he said grimly, scrubbing his chest and arms with sand mixed with water.

"We will cross at Hazoua then," Rick said decisively. "It is not too far from Nefta if we need help and being a desert post, they will not be expecting any trouble. We will tell them that this is one of our team who has lost his passport, if they ask. If they do not we will simply bribe them to let him through. We will drive before first light in the morning, and if we are lucky, cross at dusk when they are saying their prayers."

"And hope that Allah is with us," Brahim breathed fervently. "And that he looks with favor upon this plan." He looked at Robbie now lying on the bank of the pond seemingly lifeless.

"But Allah knows that a man will risk his life for his son and that is good in his sight. So may he protect us." Brahim, cleansed by the water and sand, turned toward Mecca and began to say his prayers.

Rick sat, watching the seemingly lifeless body of his son, and wondering if he would ever be whole and alive again. He was filled with a deep sense of despair and disgust at what men do in the name of warfare.

Chapter Fourteen

Janine awoke with a start from a fitful dream in which she was trying to get somewhere in the dark, but kept opening the wrong door. Then she heard the light tapping on her window. She pulled the curtain aside to see Ahmed's swarthy face grinning at her. Hanz was snoring heavily, still tied to the chair.

She let Ahmed into the room, and while he untied Hanz, she changed her clothes and tucked her gun into a holster under her arm, covering it with a loose shirt. She wasn't sure how much she trusted Ahmed to protect her if the going got rough.

They forced a groggy and protesting Hanz out the door and into the pre-dawn light. Sea birds were swooping and crying as they awoke and began their day-long search for food. Hanz stumbled in the sand, his hands still tied behind his back, and Janine heard Ahmed curse under his breath.

The German was clearly doing his best not to cooperate. Suddenly he straightened up and began to walk faster, with Ahmed's pistol in the small of his back. He was like a reluctant teenager being forced to go to school. Only this walk on the beach had far more serious consequences.

After about half a mile, he stopped and looked around. Then he told Ahmed something in a whiney voice, which Janine could barely understand. Ahmed looked at him in disgust and then translated.

"He says that we need a boat to get there. It is on the other side of the island and he will only recognize the place from the water."

"I think that he's stalling," Janine said grimly. "But I did see him and von Grantz being picked up by a boat the first day we were here. And they did go around the coast somewhere. But he may still be stalling."

"The only way to find out is to get a boat," Ahmed said, tucking his gun into his belt. "Keep him out of trouble until I get back. There is a small power boat moored behind the hotel for the guest's use. Are you armed?" Janine nodded.

Ahmed winked at her. "Most commercial attaches are, I've noticed," he said smugly. Janine resisted an impulse to kick him. Instead, she trained her pistol on the now blubbering Hanz, whom she backed against a tree.

"Please hurry back. I don't want to shoot him before we find the *machina*," she said, loudly enough for the German to hear. Then she backed him behind a rock, and made him sit facing her, in case some early morning beach sweepers or peanut vendors should wander by. But the beach was still deserted. The light had just begun to break and the soft waves lapping at the beach gave off a hissing sound. The morning smelled of salt and sea vegetation. Otherwise all was silence.

Finally, there was the far off sound of an outboard motor and Ahmed came into view, steering a flat bottomed skiff, such as the fishermen used. It was painted bright blue, with a fading red line around its bow. Ahmed maneuvered it close enough to the beach so that Janine and the German could climb aboard, but not without Hanz almost capsizing them in the process.

Ahmed finally grabbed him by his belt and hauled him aboard backwards, like a sack of potatoes. Then he gunned the motor and took them far enough from land so that the German's cries couldn't be heard.

The salt air felt fresh and clean and for a moment Janine felt almost happy. Perhaps they were nearing the end of this twisting skein of mystery. If the German would only cooperate, they might soon have one of the major pieces of the puzzle.

Ahmed was watching Hanz closely. Now that they were out of sight of the hotel complex, they were cruising along deserted beaches. Most of them were flat and sandy, with no place where anything could be hidden, unless it was buried somewhere in the sand.

Soon they were approaching a series of small islands, really no more than sandbars sticking out of the Mediterranean, like marbles that a child had let fall carelessly from his pocket. Hanz's eyes were lidded. He had hunched down in the front of the boat and was trying to shade his face from the sun with his manacled hands.

Ahmed slowed the boat and cautiously circled the islands. One of them had a simple structure on it, such as a fisherman might have built.

"Let's leave the German here," he said to Janine. "By the time they find him he will be dead of thirst or starvation."

The German rolled his eyes and made strangling sounds. Then he began to cry again and in between his sobs he said, "I vill show you, I vill show you." He struggled to get to his feet and pointed with his bound hands.

"It is there on the *kline* island."

He indicated the smallest island of the group, which was also the highest out of the water. There were several heavy rocks in the middle of it which didn't look as though they were there naturally.

Ahmed eased the boat over to the little island and after taking out fishing tackle, which he handed to Janine and Hanz for cover, jumped out of the boat and began to dig cautiously around the rocks with a small shovel.

"Keep your eyes open and look like you are fishing," he ordered Janine, over his shoulder. "We may just have hit pay dirt, as you Americans say."

Just then, his shovel hit something metallic. He dug furiously for a few minutes and the edges of a metal box, about the size of a small suitcase, began to appear. He glanced around cautiously.

They were still alone in the early morning. The lapping of the waves on the sandy beach was the only sound. Janine was keeping a weather eye on Hanz, who held a fishing rod in his manacled hands.

Ahmed made a quick decision and uncovered the rest of the box. Better to take it now and risk discovery, than to leave it here for Bonet and his men to find. There was no way that they were going to be able to keep Hanz quiet, short of killing him, and he had a feeling that Janine would hesitate to participate in that solution. He would have to take care of that himself, quietly.

He used a piece of driftwood to dislodge the metal briefcase from the sand. It had no markings, but was closed with a complicated security device that he hesitated to tamper with without expert help. He glanced at Janine, who was watching him suspiciously.

"Get in the boat, and let's get out of here," she said. "I don't want to give whoever this belongs to a chance to catch up with us out here. Our position is, in military terms, 'indefensible'."

Ahmed smiled a tiger's grin and heaved the briefcase into the boat. He then ordered Hanz to sit on it, for cover, which the hefty German did with great trepidation.

Ahmed pushed the fishing boat off the sandbar and gunned the motor. The sun was getting higher and hotter as they made their way back towards the hotel.

"What do you intend to do with this now that we've got it?" Janine asked.

"Keep it, perhaps for trading purposes," the Arab replied. "These have quite a high value on the arms market."

"And my country expressly forbids their export," Janine said firmly, assuming her role of Commercial Attaché.

"But my dear lady, you forget perhaps that we are not in your country, and here in the Arab world a nuclear triggering device is more than worth its weight in gold. There are many regimes that would pay more than that just to be the first to possess one."

"Including your own government?" Janine said, grimly.

Ahmed shook his head. "You know that we are a peace loving people, and that such things are illegal here. But many of our neighbors are not so particular."

He smiled his charming smile. "As a matter of fact, unless I miss my guess, this was intended for one of them."

He pointed the boat toward the open sea and increased the throttle of the old outboard motor.

Janine reached for her pistol, but Ahmed was too fast for her. He lunged the boat sideways so that she briefly lost her balance, and in that moment, he had his own gun trained on her.

"Let us not play this game, if you wish to live. I could explain the death of this other German. But two deaths in one day might be harder to explain."

His eyes were dark and as hard as marbles, as he looked at her and kept the gun pointed at her head.

Hanz raised from his lethargy by the hint of his possible demise, swung at Ahmed with his clenched fists, hitting him on the shoulder and causing him to lose his balance for a second. Janine took that second to grab his wrist and turn the pistol towards the sea. With an oath, Ahmed released the tiller for a moment, and hit her full in the face, causing her to fall to the bottom of the boat, hitting her head on a seat.

Hanz lost his balance and was thrown into the water screaming, "*Ich kan nicht* swimming, help *mir.*"

Janine grabbed for the briefcase and would have heaved it after him, had Ahmed not stopped her by grabbing it from her and sitting on it, while he ran the boat in circles around the thrashing German. Hanz was just about to go down for the third time, when Janine managed to toss him a life preserver. The fat German grabbed it, sobbing and paddled his way toward the boat. Ahmed again gunned the motor and left him behind in the water screaming for help.

"Was that smart?" Janine asked when she again caught her breath. "If they find his drowned body, there will be questions."

"He is to fat to drown. Besides, you thoughtfully provided him with a life preserver. If he paddles towards the shore, he will soon be able to wade in. And since he is of no further use to us, it will give me time to get rid of this 'luggage' before it falls into the wrong hands."

"Will you report this to your superior officers, as I am to mine?," Janine asked, hoping to flush out his allegiances.

Ahmed looked at her speculatively, as he lit a dark cigarette. "That, my dear lady, depends upon whom you are reporting to. I will do with the information what seems best to me. One can have many allegiances in this world. And sometimes the first one is to oneself, and one's family."

He took a long drag on the cigarette, and looked at her narrowly through the smoke. "The conditions in the Libyan prisons are less than perfect. Let it suffice to say that I have a close relative there. This instrument may buy his freedom," he said, patting the briefcase.

"And you would put the future of this part of the world at risk, to save one person from prison?," Janine asked in disbelief. "You would help to give the Libyans the power to blow their neighbors off the face of the globe?"

"If not now, then later," Ahmed said, with a shrug. "At the moment, this will only be another toy to them. A symbol of technological power which they are still unable to use. But if it will buy a brother's life, it is worth it to me."

He pointed his gun at her once more. "If you try to take it from me again, I will surely put a bullet through your head."

Janine listened to him this time. Her head ached. And far away, she could still hear Hanz crying for help. There was no mistake that this man meant what he said. For whatever reason, he was willing to kill for the triggering device. And she knew that she was not willing to die for it, not today at any rate, not this morning. She would lay low and bide her time.

At any rate, von Grantz's intended customers would not get it. And they presumably knew how to use it immediately. What she had bought for western civilization was just a little time, but not much.

She hunched low in the boat as Ahmed again gunned the motor and headed back toward the hotel. The sun was higher overhead now and there was no breeze. It was hot in the little boat, which smelled more strongly of old fish.

There was little she could do to stop Ahmed at this moment and she was grateful to still be alive.

She heard a sound which seemed to come through the bottom of the boat. It was a loud vibration, even louder than the sound of the old outboard motor and it seemed to be getting louder all the time.

She looked cautiously over the side to see a large motor boat approaching them at top speed. It was bright red and cut through the water like a knife. It looked like the kind of craft that was normally used for water skiing. But the two tough looking men in the front of the craft didn't look as though they had water skiing in mind.

Ahmed tried to point their smaller craft towards the shore, but the larger boat quickly overtook them and cut them off from escaping by land. Then they rammed the back of the fishing boat several times until they had rendered the old motor inoperable.

"Greetings friends," the taller and uglier of the men called out in French. "Come aboard and bring your luggage with you," he said, gesturing meaningfully with a semi-automatic rifle.

As Ahmed pulled his gun, the man fired one round, wounding Ahmed, and showing that he meant business. The wood of the old fishing boat splintered like cardboard and the skiff began to take on water.

Janine hunkered down in the bow with her hand on her pistol, ready to fire if they tried to haul her into the other boat.

But they were more concerned with the briefcase. One of the men spotted it and jumped into the sinking fishing boat, pushing Ahmed, whose shoulder was red with blood, into the bow with Janine.

"I've got it," he said excitedly. "This is what the boss wanted, I'm sure." He pointed his gun at Janine and Ahmed. "Shall I finish them now?"

The older man shook his head. "He wants them alive, for the moment. Let's try to keep them that way for a little while," he said, grinning evilly.

"The boat will soon sink with that many holes in her, and they will consider it a fishing accident. Too bad they came out so far without life vests," he said, pulling Janine and Ahmed into the back of the motor launch and tying their hands together with a piece of rope.

Janine's gun was still in its place. But there was no way that she could reach it with her hands tied. Ahmed had been disarmed and his shoulder was bleeding badly where it had been grazed by the automatic.

The taller of the two men stowed the briefcase under the front seat of the launch and accelerated, taking them in the opposite direction, away from the hotel.

"Thanks for doing our work for us," he said to the captives. "The boss has had us scouring the island for this briefcase for days. Nice of you to locate it for us."

Ahmed uttered an oath in Arabic which got him an ugly look from the shorter Frenchman. "Close your dirty mouth if you want to keep your teeth. I grew up in Algeria," he said, pointing his automatic directly at Ahmed. "If the boss didn't want you alive, I'd feed you to the fish right now, and your girl friend with you."

The boat was going so fast now that it was hard to see where they were headed. It kicked up a protective wave of water on both sides, which effectively shielded them from sight of anyone on land. And they were far enough out to sea that anyone seeing them would think that they were just on a pleasure cruise, or getting ready to water ski.

Janine didn't think that there would be any pleasure included in whatever was in store for them.

They finally headed towards shore on the other side of the island, towards an isolated villa which stood completely alone above a sandy beach. There was a small dock and ornamental building at the end of it.

The men quickly moored the boat and half pulled, half dragged Ahmed and Janine into this shelter. Once there, they tied their feet as well as their hands, and gagged them with some foul smelling rags.

The building was about ten feet square, perched over the water, with a ladder going down into what looked to be about six feet of water. There were no windows and only one door, which the men locked securely behind them. Janine tested her ropes and looked around for something sharp that she could use to free them. Ahmed's face was white from loss of blood, and he seemed half-stunned by what had happened to them. How had they been trapped so easily? The men must have been following them since early morning, just waiting for them to find the triggering device so they could take it from them.

Janine had managed to work her way around the post that secured her. But not much met her eyes except some low benches, and a high ornamental shelf holding decorative glass bottles. Painted wooden hooks lined the wall, one holding a white *safsari*, which looked as though it had been there for a long time.

She realized suddenly that they were in a women's bath house, constructed so that orthodox Muslim women could take a dip in the ocean without being seen by men. That explained the ladder through the floor and the lack of windows. All she could hope for was that there were some women in the house who would want to go swimming soon. Otherwise they might be trapped here for a long time.

Ahmed looked more and more as though he needed medical attention, if he was going to make it. His shoulder and arm were caked with blood, and he seemed to have fallen into a half stupor, until he suddenly looked in her direction. His eyes were alive with hatred. He looked like a wounded tiger, plotting revenge on his captors.

But hours went by and no one came, neither was there any sound outside the bath house. It was as though the men who had captured them had vanished into thin air, taking the triggering device with them. But where had they taken it?

Janine had fallen into a restless half-sleep, when she was awakened by a sound outside the building. It was two people talking in low voices. But it didn't sound like French, more like Arabic. Janine pounded her heels on the floor with all her might, which wasn't much. But she did manage to make a muffled sound.

The voices stopped. Then there was a long silence, and the door began to open a crack, letting in the afternoon light. Two pretty young girls, their faces half covered with *safsaris*, looked curiously into the room and gasped with fright at what they saw. They began to back out of the door, but Janine pounded her heels again and nodded towards the wounded Ahmed.

The girls started visibly to see a man in the bath-house, and a bloody one at that. They gasped and slammed the door behind them. Janine could hear them running up the gravel path talking excitedly.

It seemed a year before anything else happened. Ahmed's eyes were closed, and his face was gray. Janine had worn all the skin off her wrists, struggling to free them, and her mouth was so dry from the gag that each breath was torture.

She had tried kicking against the wall hoping to dislodge one of the decorative glass bottles, and had only succeeded in raising a great deal of ancient dust. Her bladder was bursting, and she began to regret how she had tortured Hanz to get him to talk.

Suddenly the door opened, and an aristocratic looking Tunisian man stood there, looking astonished and very angry at what he found in the women's private quarters of his beach home.

Some time later Janine was at the hospital with Ahmed. His military identification and rank had cut through all the formalities usually associated with a gun shot wound.

Their host Ben Youseff, after getting over his shock at finding them in his women's quarters, had been kindness itself. He had plied them with hot tea and called his personal physician to attend to Ahmed's wound.

But this man, conscious of his legal responsibilities had insisted on driving them to the local hospital.

Between them, Janine and Ahmed had concocted a cover story that seemed to have everyone temporarily convinced. They had been out fishing and had been accosted by some thieves. The men had lost their nerve, and hidden them on what they thought was a deserted estate. Ben Youseff and his family had arrived from Tunis to find them bound and gagged in his bath house. End of story.

But the triggering device was now in someone else's hands. The question was who had it, and where?

Janine waited while the Tunisian nurse fitted Ahmed with a sling for his injured shoulder and arm. The officer suffered her attentions grimly, clearly itching to be out of the hospital and pursuit of whomever had been responsible for their being "trussed up like pigs," he muttered as the small taxi drove them away from the hospital honking and narrowly avoiding both donkeys and pedestrians.

"Where to now?" Janine asked brightly, "Have you got any more good ideas?"

Ahmed glared at her, shifted his shoulder angrily, and winced with pain as he did it. "To kill the viper, or at least defang him," he said, shifting his weight to get more comfortable as the taxi sped around a curve.

"And who would that be?" Janine asked casually, reassuring herself with the feel of the revolver in her waistband.

"Those two men were Franco-Algerians, *pied noir*. So is Bonet," Ahmed grimaced. "It doesn't take brilliance to imagine that he knows the whereabouts of the triggering device, and that his thugs probably stole it for him. "He looked at Janine with a wry smile. "We too have had our eyes on this man for some time. His interest in our country is too acute not to have been noticed and followed."

"But he works for Duke Weston," Janine gasped, "one of the most respected businessmen in the United States."

"And we have always felt he was a true friend to Tunisia," Ahmed said gravely. "If what I think is true of Bonet, it will create a serious situation for the relationship between our two countries."

"Unless Weston doesn't know about it," Janine said, grasping at straws.

"That is why I must go to Bonet's villa and find the answer," Ahmed said, giving the driver some coins as they pulled up in front of the hotel.

"But not without me," Janine answered grimly. "The future diplomatic relations of our two countries may depend upon what we find there, and whether you like it or not, that is officially my concern."

Chapter Fifteen

It was a weary group of travelers that arrived at the little desert town of El Oued late in the afternoon. Rick had driven the Jeep without stopping even to eat or drink tea, much to Brahim's disgust. Robbie slept in the back seat, waking now and then to look around fearfully and then to drop back into a deep sleep, punctuated by moans and half garbled Arabic words.

"The bandits have put the evil eye on him," Brahim said solemnly. "They have taken his reason from him. It is their revenge."

Rick made an impatient gesture. "There is no such thing as the evil eye and you know it. The boy has just been frightened and tortured out of his mind, but he will get better once we get him back to some medical help." He started to say 'civilization', but then thought better of it. The Arab civilization was older than his own and was now involved in a kind of ethnic cleansing in Algeria that mirrored the atrocities of the Nazis in Germany. Reasonable men seemed helpless to stop it now, as then. He felt old and tired. He had stopped thinking about what his company must be doing without word of him for days. Hopefully he could make it right when he was finally able to get in touch with them. But Robbie was alive, if not yet in his right mind, and for the moment, that was all that mattered.

The border crossing seemed deserted except for one lone sentry who looked only nervous at their approach. Brahim called out to him first and then offered him a cigarette. The young man seemed anxious to talk, and he and Brahim had soon struck up a lively conversation in Arabic. Brahim pointed to the Jeep and gestured graphically indicating that they had someone who was not quite right in the head with them. The sentry nodded nervously and held out his hand for another cigarette. While he smoked it, Brahim strolled casually back to the Jeep.

"I think that it can be done, if we add more cigarettes and some Algerian *backshis*. He has been left here alone 'til tomorrow, and he fears that the bandits will come. They are now attacking further and further from Algiers. No one knows who will be next and he is afraid that it will be him." The young police officer smiled engagingly. "Besides he feels that to be touched by madness is the will of Allah, and that your son must be protected, if not honored. He will let us through. But the Tunisians may not be so easy to convince."

Rick sped through the crossing point before the young guard had time to change his mind. They left him with the rest of their Algerian money, a pack of cigarettes and a smile on his face. He would tell his children that honoring the madness of the boy had brought him good fortune. This is how legends are made.

They bumped along the dusty road in the dying light. Ahead of them, they could just see the faint lights of Nefta, the Tunisian crossing point. Brahim insisted on stopping first by the side of the road, making tea and changing into his policeman's uniform. It was crumpled and dusty, but still recognizable. He seemed to take on another persona wearing it. Almost as though he grew taller. "If worst comes to worst, I shall tell them that I have arrested you both." He grinned, "That should be a good enough story to get us through the crossing and back to Tozeur and my chief. He will be proud that I have rescued your son and brought you back alive."

There was a long line of people waiting before them at the Nefta crossing. The Tunisian authorities were taking their time inspecting each passport and going through everyone's luggage very carefully.

Most of the other tourists were young and travel worn, clearly eager to get out of Algeria and back to the relative security of Tunisia. Rick overheard snippets of conversation which made him realize just how lucky they had been. But these inveterate desert travelers related their adventures with gusto, seemingly oblivious to the danger they had placed themselves in. "Almost a thousand people killed in the villages around Algiers", one grubby blonde young man related casually. "Seemed as good a time as any to get out of there."

The Tunisian border guard looked at him with something like pity. "Only a stupid man goes into Algeria now if it isn't necessary. They kill there for pleasure. It is against the Koran, but the bandits do it anyhow. Only Allah knows where it all will end."

He inspected Rick's passport carefully and looked into the Jeep, and at Robbie, with suspicion. Only Brahim's story and his policeman's uniform and papers finally got them through, but not without a long wait while a call was placed to the chief of police in Tozeur. After what seemed an interminable conversation they finally let them go, reluctantly. Rick again thanked his lucky stars and gunned the Jeep towards Tozeur.

Brahim swelled with pride to have gotten them through the border. He was loquacious now that they were nearing home. He clearly saw himself as the hero of the adventure. Not even Robbie's confused ramblings in the back seat seemed to disturb him now. They tore at Rick's heart. But he took solace in the fact that the boy no longer seemed afraid of him. Only lost in a world of his own.

The lights of Tozeur twinkled dimly in the distance. Rick was almost as delighted as Brahim was to see them. They meant warm food and a bed and, with any luck, a telephone that worked. For the first time, he thought about Janine in D'Jerba and wondered how her mission was going. It seemed a year since he had left her to search for Robbie. He wondered briefly if she was all right and if she needed help.

They found the hotel still open and the proprietor half asleep behind his desk. Brahim left them to report to his chief, and for the first time

Rick was left alone with Robbie. He decided against trying to eat with him in public and instead took some soup up to the room they shared. He locked the door as a precaution before he left, and returned to find Robbie sitting in the middle of the bed where he had left him. His hands held in front of him as if bound and his head hanging. At first he thought that the boy was asleep, but as he entered, Robbie screamed and tried to strike out at him, with a pitiful blow that Rick managed to deflect without spilling the soup.

After looking at it for a moment suspiciously, the boy grabbed the bowl and slurped it down like an animal. Then he whimpered and fell back on the bed and curled into a fetal position.

Rick covered him with a rough blanket and sat beside him until he fell asleep. Then he went downstairs again and placed two calls, one to his office and one to Sam. The office call was predictable. They were angry at not having heard from him, but ready to forgive if he delivered some new business from the area soon.

Sam was another matter. His voice was controlled but his message was not. Janine was carrying out the assignment alone and was probably in trouble. Rick had not upheld his part of the bargain. It was imperative that he get to D'Jerba as soon as possible and give her what help he could. This all couched in the most polite of business language. But Rick got the point. He squelched an angry retort, and simply replied. "I have found the missing package. It is not in very good condition and may need extensive repairs. I suggest you let the interested parties know." Duke and Melanie would have to be satisfied for now with that much information.

"The other package may be permanently lost if you don't hurry", was Sam's only reply. "I have been unable to supply any backup from here." Then the telephone went dead. No amount of coaxing would get it to make another call. The few lights in Tozeur had gone out by now. Rick was loathe to leave Robbie alone in the hotel, in case he awoke screaming or tried to leave the room. He decided to pack it in for the night, and leave early in the morning for D'Jerba. By plane if possible.

Robbie seemed somewhat better in the morning. He was docile and ate his breakfast ravenously. He still did not speak intelligibly or seem to recognize Rick, but he had lost some of the haunted look in his eyes, and the rope burns on his wrists had begun to heal.

Rick called the local Air Tunis office and booked two seats on the afternoon plane to D'Jerba. He then called the Embassy in Tunis to locate where Janine and her party were staying. Fortunately Janine's secretary remembered him and gave him the information in an "I really shouldn't do this" voice. He thanked her profusely, and promised to bring her a gift from the desert. Then he locked Robbie in the room again and went out to try to find some clothes that fit him for the journey. He also needed to dispose of the Jeep at the local car rental. The attendant demanded a large bonus for taking it back in what he claimed was terrible condition. Rick grimly paid the fine and jogged back to the hotel, cursing rental agencies under his breath.

He found the hotel manager in a state of agitation. Robbie was pounding on the door and screaming. Rick explained that the boy was his son, and had recently been through an emotional trauma. The manager looked at him with crafty eyes, and explained that what Rick did was his own business, but that he should take the boy somewhere else to do it. His was an honorable hotel. Rick paid for the room, and then put another dinar into the manager's outstretched hand, and then another. Then he ran up the steps to his room, where he found a distraught Robbie hunched against the door, crying.

He helped the boy to take a warm shower and to put on his new clothes. The khaki pants and tee shirt hung loosely on his angular frame. His reddish hair had grown long and thick and there was the beginning of a soft stubble of beard on his chin. His blue eyes were still vacant as though looking at something far away. Rick began to suspect that he had been severely drugged, and that the effects of whatever it was had not yet worn off. However, the boy seemed calmer when Rick was with him and he allowed himself to be washed and dressed without protest.

Rick decided to feed him again before they left on the airplane. He walked with him to the *Restaurant du Paradis*, just a few blocks from the hotel. The streets were now full of tourists descending from the local tour busses. Camel drivers hawked rides on their disdainful looking camels and teen-agers rode rented motor bikes through the streets. Robbie shuffled along at Rick's side, looking neither to the right or left. He didn't react until a plate of chicken cous cous was put before him along with a large coca cola. He began to eat it with his fingers, hungrily, and downed the coke in one draught. Two teen-agers at an adjacent table snickered loudly when Rick gently put a fork into Robbie's hand and showed him how to use it. The boy reacted strangely, first looking at it as though he had never seen one before, and then smiling shyly at Rick as he began to eat again rapidly.

The cous cous was followed with a pastry dripping honey and almonds, and two cups of black Arab coffee. The fat proprietor brought the coffee himself and smiled at Rick like an old friend. He included Robbie in his oozing warmth.

"So you have found a friend in the oasis. That is good. Welcome again to Tozeur my friend. May you return many times." Rick paid the bill and tipped him generously. He was beginning to experience a feeling of relief. Robbie was here with him. And with every minute that passed, he was looking more like himself, though his mind was still somewhere else. The young had amazing powers of recuperation.

Rick hailed a taxi. He picked up his bags at the hotel and gave the driver instructions to take them to the small desert airport to catch the one plane to D'Jerba that day. As they bumped along the road, Rick caught sight of a police car following them. When they reached the airport, the car pulled in behind them and the police chief and Brahim got out. The chief waved the taxi driver on and then took Rick by the arm and led him to a side entrance. Brahim led a struggling Robbie after them.

The chief looked at Rick seriously. "This is not good my friend. You did not come this morning to thank me or to introduce your son.

Remember that I told you we suspect that he was helping to smuggle narcotics. The other two boys have been caught in D'Jerba and I should hold your son too as an accomplice."

Robbie had now begun to struggle and to moan and Brahim was having a problem holding on to him. Robbie's long reddish blonde hair had fallen into his eyes which were like those of a hunted animal. He fell to his knees on the cement screaming and crying.

The chief looked taken aback. He crossed over to Robbie and examined the burn marks on his wrists and the angry welts on his neck which his long hair had covered. Brahim pulled the boy to his feet and showed the chief the marks on his ankles. The chief nodded wordlessly. Then he looked at Rick and said seriously. "It seems that the boy has been punished enough. From what Brahim tells me he may bear the marks of his visit to Algeria all his life. We will not add to it a Tunisian punishment." He held out his hand to Rick. "Go, and may Allah protect you both. I have not seen you this morning."

As the plane took off from the runway, Rick could see them both standing by the police car. Their figures grew minuscule as the plane lifted into the bumpy air warmed by the afternoon's heat. Tozeur grew smaller and smaller below them, a scattering of houses on the edge of the dusky green of the oasis which cut into the ocher of the desert like a benediction.

Robbie slept, strapped into his seat next to the window. Rick again felt a strange calm. Whatever lay ahead of him in D'Jerba he could manage as long as he had found his son. He felt as though for the first time in weeks he was breathing normally. A knot in his chest unclenched and he felt almost lighthearted as he accepted a drink from the jasmine scented attendant.

His fellow passengers were mostly tourists, Scandinavians and Germans looking for the spring sun in the desert and in the fabled island of D'Jerba. There was a holiday mood on the little plane and for the first time in weeks, Rick felt himself relax and almost look forward to what lay ahead. It would be good to see Janine again and give her any help he could, if she would accept it.

*   *   *

Janine had managed to persuade Ahmed to wait until evening to go to Bonet's villa. His aching arm was one part of the quotient, as was Melanie's fluttering concern. She had immediately claimed Ahmed as her patient, and had him stretched out beside her on a chaise lounge beside the pool. She was plying him with cold drinks and sandwiches, which she ordered from the kitchen and insisted on feeding him, while making clucking noises of concern. Her tiny bikini didn't make her look like any nurse that Janine had ever seen. But Janine was delighted to have the officer occupied while she made plans for the evening assault on Bonet's villa.

Hanz had showed up earlier in the day, sunburned and taciturn. He kept shooting withering glances in Janine's direction. But she blithely ignored him while trying to figure out how to get into Bonet's villa without being seen. She had noticed numerous servants about the house, some of them half-veiled women wearing the *safsari*. The billowing white garment would make a good disguise. If she could keep her head down and her mouth shut. She might just get away with it.

She called Bonet's villa and was told that he was not in, but that he was hosting a party for some film people that evening and would surely return by six o'clock. She changed her plan on the spot and decided to ask Melanie to call him to get them all invited to the party. There was safety in numbers and in the confusion of a large and glamorous party, maybe one more Arab serving woman wouldn't be noticed.

Melanie went for the idea immediately, while Ahmed looked daggers in Janine's direction. Melanie was on her cell phone and tracking Bonet down like a practiced sleuth. Janine wondered for a moment if perhaps she had missed her calling. Her tones turned to honey when she finally reached him and received an invitation for all four of them.

He was hosting a film crew who were shooting in the desert, and the leading man was a particular favorite of Melanie's. She forgot about Ahmed and his wound in her excitement over what she was going to wear that evening.

Janine knew what she was going to wear. Whatever it was, was going to have to be easily covered with the *safsari* that she folded into a large handbag. She added the pistol, which obviously wasn't going to fit under her evening attire. She decided to fill Brian in on what was going on in case she had to disappear during the evening and for some reason didn't return.

Brian was delighted to be asked back to the villa. Bonet had an extraordinary collection of Arab antiquities, and he was anxious to have another look at them. Besides it was amusing to watch Melanie try to work her wiles on Bonet. Brian was almost sure that he didn't prefer women if a choice were given. Some of the antiquities were pretty erotic when studied carefully.

Only Ahmed was not delighted with Janine's plan. "We troop in there like a tribe of monkeys on display, and what do you suppose we will find?" he asked Janine angrily, with one arm pushing himself to a seated position on the lounge, while trying to reach for a cigarette with the other.

"More than we will find if the two of us try to sneak in there together," she replied, lighting the cigarette for him. "You are not exactly in top form to do battle. And from what we've seen of his troops, they out weigh us and out gun us. How about trying a little diversionary action, instead of marching up to his front door and demanding that he hand over the triggering device?"

"If it's even still there," Ahmed said glumly.

"That's a chance we have to take don't we?" Janine replied. "I don't think that he would risk sending it out as unaccompanied luggage. Which means that he probably means to take it out himself on his private plane that leaves tomorrow, I'm told." At Ahmed's surprised look she responded. "Just a little more of Melanie's intelligence work. That woman is a wonder when she wants something."

Ahmed nodded wryly in agreement and moved to ease his shoulder. "So then what is your plan?" he asked. When Janine told him he almost laughed in her face. "You posing as an Arab cleaning woman. They will throw you out or kill you on the spot if they find you snooping around."

"Not if the Tunisian military provide adequate back up," Janine replied. "Besides, have you got a better idea?"

"Not at the moment," Ahmed answered grimly. "But I'm thinking about it."

The party that entered Bonet's house that evening was dressed to the nines. Ahmed had put on his dress uniform with his wounded arm in a sling, into which he had slipped small revolver. Melanie had decided to deck herself out in a shimmering golden caftan she had bought in an exclusive shop in the bazaar. She looked quite lovely in it. And her face was flushed with anticipation at the prospect of meeting one of her favorite movie stars.

Janine wore a simple white caftan with gold trim and large hoop earrings. She had pulled her hair back into a chignon to make it easier to disguise it under the *safsari* should the occasion arise. Brian was in his usual uniform of khaki pants and a navy blue jacket with brass buttons. But he wore a serious look on his usually cheerful face. Janine had thought about arming him, but had decided against it. Shooting their way out of Bonet's villa was probably their last option. Surprise and safety in numbers was probably their best advantage. Having Duke Weston's daughter with them might give them some protection.

They rang the bell to the ornate front door. A servant answered, dressed in a spotless white jacket with gold buttons. He led them into the atrium in the center of the house where a group of Tunisian musicians played antique stringed instruments. The sound of the *oud*, the *rubeck* and a violin, mingled with the fountain's cool sounds.

Bonet greeted them warmly and complimented Melanie and Janine on their "Arab attire". "How amusing for our guests from Hollywood to see two such beautiful ladies going native," he said with a slight smile. Melanie's face fell, and Janine resisted the urge to hit him in his perfect white teeth.

She was restrained by Ahmed's look and also by the arrival of the Hollywood party. The producer was a fat little man with a habitually worried look. The famous blonde actor with his perfect profile, was wearing jeans and a tee shirt, and looking as though he would rather be anywhere else but at a cocktail party.

Several other members of the cast and crew drifted in and, after drinks were passed around, the atmosphere lightened a bit. Melanie sauntered over to the handsome young actor and soon had him backed up against a flowering shrub, while she fluttered her eyes, and paid him compliments. He seemed to relax after a few moments and almost smiled at her. He clearly enjoyed the adulation of women.

At a look from Janine, Brian edged his way politely into the circle standing around Bonet. When there was a break in the conversation, Brian asked him about his collection of Arab art. Bonet looked at him strangely for a moment and then, after Brian made a few knowledgeable remarks, offered to show it to him later after dinner.

"Oh, you're busy with your guests. Mind if I just wander around and look at things. I have a pretty good collection of my own," he lied charmingly.

With the other guests looking at him expectantly, there was nothing that Bonet could do but agree. Brian gave him his best Virginia gentleman smile of thanks and wandered out of the room, stopping to admire the intricate design of blue and yellow tiles over the door. Janine watched him leave, delighted at his savoir faire.

Brian wandered through the rooms, checking them quickly as Janine had asked him to, for anything that looked as though it might be a concealed hiding place. The rooms were almost bare of furniture. Bonet seemed to prefer to give most of the space to his works of art, which were an eclectic collection of old and new. Recessed lights showed off fragments of Greek and Roman statuary, as well as a few modern paintings and some beautiful Arab ornamental calligraphy. Most of the rooms opened back into the courtyard, where the party was taking place, and Brian smiled and waved as he emerged each time from another treasure room. All the doors were easy to open, except one in the last room, which led to the traditional tower on the ocean side of the building. This door was locked firmly. A white garbed servant came in as he was trying it casually.

"No good, no good," the man said firmly, pulling Brian away from the door. "You go back to party now, dinner ready."

Brian went out into the courtyard, blinking into the last rays of the sun. The party was in full swing now and Janine was nowhere to be seen. There were at least thirty people in the courtyard and the party had begun to spill into the living room and dining room. He found Janine in a corner of the dining room deep in conversation with Ahmed.

"There's not much of a place to hide anything," Brian reported. The place is like a museum. He must have been collecting for years."

"Or stealing, our antiquities," Ahmed retorted.

"At any rate, the only thing that I found that looks promising is a door that leads to that tower at the back of the building. Most of the D'Jerban houses have them. A servant warned me off when I tried the door. If he's hiding something here, I'll bet you that's where it is."

He coughed and nodded toward two of the guests that had joined them in the dining room. "His collection is really spectacular", he continued in his best University of Virginia voice. "Maybe he'll take you all on a tour after dinner."

"Or perhaps I will try to take a look while you are all having dinner," Janine said, under her breath. "If Bonet asks where I am, tell him that I felt ill and had to go home. I will sneak back in through the servant's entrance and see what I can find."

"That's perhaps the craziest idea I've ever heard," Ahmed said through his teeth. "If he catches you, and he will catch you, we may never see you again."

"And you would just hate that, wouldn't you?" Janine retorted. If you have a better idea, tell me now."

The tall Arab was silent as Janine waved him a saucy goodbye, and slipped out the door to put on her *safsari*.

Brian watched her go with trepidation. His gentlemanly instincts told him that she shouldn't be allowed to go this alone. But he had absolutely no idea of what to do to stop her.

Chapter Sixteen

Rick and Robbie had arrived at the D'Jerba airport late that afternoon. Rick deliberately chose a small hotel on the other side of town from the main tourist area and far enough away from the hotel where he knew Janine and her group were staying. He wanted a chance to get the lay of the land before he announced himself, and there remained the problem of what to do about Robbie. He wanted to get in touch with a decent local doctor if one existed. And because Robbie lacked a passport and tourist visa, he needed to get in touch with the Embassy as soon as possible and see what could be done to get papers expedited for him. For the moment, as far as the Tunisians were concerned anyway, Robbie was a non-person.

They holed up in a third-rate tourist hotel filled with back-packers where Robbie's condition was less apt to be remarked on. Most of the people staying there were young Germans and Scandinavians on vacation in search of the spring sun. They were casually dressed, young and boisterous. Robbie seemed to relax a bit in their presence. He looked less haunted, like someone emerging from a long sleep. He still didn't recognize Rick, but he no longer seemed afraid of him. And he ate voraciously at every opportunity.

It was almost evening by the time Rick again reached Sam in Paris and found out what was going on with Janine. He reported cautiously on Robbie's condition, knowing for a fact that the line was probably not secure. Sam had reached Duke Weston with the news of Robbie's rescue. His orders, relayed by Sam, were to finish the mission as soon as possible, and then get Robbie out of the country and to a specialist.

But what kind of specialist? Rick wondered grimly. He no longer recognized the lanky youngster as his son. He was full of long silences and seemed to move in a kind of dream-like state. Rick wasn't sure if this was the result of drugs or shock or a combination of the two. But he was very loathe to leave the boy alone for long while he went searching for Janine and her crew. And he was sure that he couldn't take Robbie boy along with him, he was too unstable.

Part of the solution presented itself at dinner in the small cafe next door. Two Norwegian looking, blonde young men were playing the flute and guitar and singing for coins. Robbie seemed fascinated by the music, tapping his feet and listening with an intensity that was new behavior. Rick gave the boys a dinar and invited them over to their table. They played some more songs and seemed to take for granted Robbie's spaced out condition. Robbie continued to nod his head and tap on the table in time to the music.

"Had a bad trip did he?" one of the boys asked sympathetically. "Happened to my brother last year. It was really a bad scene for a couple of days. We had to watch him all the time. Afraid that he would kill himself." There was real sympathy in his eyes as he played for Robbie. "He kind of reminds me of my brother."

"He's had a real bad time," Rick agreed. "And I am afraid to leave him alone, but I need to do some things tonight, and I need someone to keep an eye on him and perhaps play him some music and see that he eats. Are you two available for hire."

"Yeah, but we don't do drugs," the boys answered solemnly.

"He's probably had enough drugs to last him a lifetime," Rick answered. "I just need someone I can trust to keep and eye on him for a few hours and keep him out of trouble. I'll pay you more than you make in an evening when I get back."

The boys looked at one another, considering. "But what if you don't come back?" they asked. "Then what do we do with him."

Rick was liking the young man more and more. "In that unlikely event, call the American Embassy in Tunis and they will come and get him. But don't worry, I'll be back. He's my son." Rick checked their ID's, and paid them enough in advance to keep them playing for awhile. Robbie didn't seem to notice that he was leaving. He had a half smile on his face and now his whole body was moving slightly to the lilting music. Rick remembered that he had once played the guitar. Perhaps the music reminded him of an earlier, happier time.

Rick grabbed one of the ever-present tourist cabs and made it to Janine's hotel in record time, only to find that the whole party was out for the evening. The manager was only too eager to regale him with all the unfortunate events of the last few days, beginning with the death of von Grantz, and the "accidental" shooting of Ahmed. Hanz wandered in during the recounting of the story and, clearly happy to see a fellow scientist, told him his side of the woeful tale. He also said that the party had left him behind when they went to visit with the film stars at Bonet's house that evening. In response to Rick's questioning, he also supplied the location.

Rick hesitated for just a few moments. It was imperative that he get in touch with Janine as soon as possible. Something that Sam had told him in confidence indicated that their time might be running out. But he was very loathe to leave Robbie for that long with the two musicians. He gave the manager the phone number of his hotel and asked the man to have Janine call him as soon as she returned, no matter how late it was. Then he commiserated with Hanz for a few more minutes and eventually got most of the story of his "kidnaping." It sounded like unlikely behavior for Janine and Ahmed, unless there was much more to it than Hanz was telling him, and he suspected that there was, much more. Besides Hanz looked unharmed, except for a blistering sun burn which, although it was probably uncomfortable, certainly wasn't fatal.

He found Robbie unharmed, considerably more relaxed, and still in the restaurant. The boys, Ty and Erik, had stood him to a pizza with their earnings, and they had even let him hold the guitar and strum along during one of their numbers. For just a moment Rick caught a familiar glimpse of his son—long reddish blonde hair half covering his face, a wispy beard and a half smile as he bent over the guitar. But his blue eyes were still clouded and showed no signs of recognition as he glanced at his father. He stood up obediently when Rick told him that they had to leave, gave back the guitar and nodded at his new friends. There was no sign of the old rebellious Robbie, only a troubling passivity.

"Stay cool man," Ty said, patting him on the shoulder. He glanced sympathetically at Rick. "Takes time to get over a really bad trip, but he's a good guy. Give him time." He looked down at his friend holding the guitar. "My brother killed himself, when we weren't watching. So you know to keep an eye on him 'til he comes out of it."

"I know", Rick said gratefully." Are you guys going to be around tomorrow? I may need someone to watch him while I go and help a friend?"

The young men looked at each other for a moment. Then Erik shrugged. "We were moving on to Gabes, but we can hang around another day if it would help you out. The tips are good here," he said fingering the dinars that Rick had given him. "And besides he plays a pretty good guitar," he added, nodding towards Robbie. He gave Rick the name of the youth hostel where they were staying. "Call us before ten if you need us. We help clean up the place and then they want us all out right after that, no hanging around."

Rick felt an intense sense of relief having found someone to watch over Robbie. The young men had a healthy look about them, and Robbie obviously responded to their music.

There was nothing that he could do now but go back to the room and hope to hear soon from Janine. Once he knew that she was all right, he was going to hop the next plane to Tunis and find some expert help for Robbie.

*   *   *

Janine had slipped away from the party, without Bonet or the other guests noticing. They were all too enthralled with the handsome young movie star to pay much attention to one female American guest. Janine had counted on the glamour of the evening to work in her favor. She slipped on the *safsari*, which covered her like a tent, adjusted her veil, and changed her high heels for Arab sandals. It was fortunate for her that some of the D'Jerban women still went veiled. In Tunis she might have been noticed. Here, the more conservative D'Jerban custom was her protection, temporarily.

She hid her bag in the bushes, but took her pistol with her. She also took a small tool kit that would enable her to pick a number of locks, especially old cumbersome metal ones. Brian had reported that the door to the tower was an ornate old one. These were often locked with antique keys, and the mechanism were not too difficult to trip if one knew how. Janine thanked her early CIA training. This was something that she had not done in a long time.

She heard a sound and pressed herself against the shadowy side of the building. In typical D'Jerban style there were no windows on the outside walls, and as far as she could tell, only one other entrance on this side of the building. It was open and light spilled out of it, revealing baskets of vegetables and some empty wine crates. She peered in cautiously, and saw a dimly lighted passageway leading to the servant's quarters and the kitchen. She picked up one of the baskets of vegetables as her cover, and made her way cautiously into the half-lighted corridor. Through an open door, she could see the white garbed cook putting the last touches on the evening meal.

He was screaming at several waiters over some infraction as he loaded their serving dishes with the first course. Janine took advantage of the confusion to slip by the open door unnoticed, and to make her way around to the other side of the building, to the entrance of the mysterious locked tower.

Two men sat in the room now, smoking and guarding the door. Further evidence that something important must be inside. They were relaxed and talking quietly in Arabic. Janine froze outside the door; then backed quietly down the hallway. There had to be some way to create a diversion, anything to get them out of the room long enough so that she could try her magic pick on the door. One of them stretched and walked into the hall, and looked both ways. Then he returned to his idle conversation. A bell rang somewhere in the vicinity of the kitchen. It rang again imperiously, as though summoning the world to something important.

The men exited from the room laughing. Janine, hidden in the shadows, could see that they were wearing serving coats. They must be extra help called in to serve at the party, and not guards as she had supposed. They passed her in the corridor, not even acknowledging her presence, as was customary with Arab males.

She slid quickly into the room. The light was low and came from special lamps fixed on the displayed antiquities. Even to Janine's unpracticed eye it was clear that Bonet owned a great number of fine Tunisian antiquities. She wondered briefly if they had been bought or stolen. One statue in particular caught her eye. It was of a young Greek boy, finely wrought and almost intact. It was mounted on a slender pedestal and stood in the middle of the room. Lights from above and below outlined the boy's beauty, as he stood in a relaxed pose with one knee thrust forward, a spear in one hand. It must be one of the prizes of Bonet's collection and belonged in a museum.

She dared not try for more light, so she huddled by the antique door to the tower, working quickly with one of her lock-picks. The old metal lock had been replaced with a more modern one. Fortunately it was well oiled and easy to probe. She could hear a clicking sound which told her that she had reached the mechanism, but the lock refused to open. She stood back and took a deep breath and tried again, more slowly. This time the mechanism clicked and the door gave a little when she turned the handle. Then it opened into a pitch black corridor.

She closed the door behind her, leaving it ever so slightly ajar. Now she was in total blackness. She could feel rocky walls on both sides of her. They were cool to her touch and rough, as though chiseled by hand long ago. She stood still for a moment waiting for her eyes to become accustomed to the blackness. Now, far above her, she could see a patch of gray, as though a window might be open. She began to climb the stairs cautiously, hugging the wall for support. She cursed herself for not bringing a flashlight, but it was too late now.

The stairs curved upwards, and she realized that the gray spot that she had seen was just light at the top of the stairs. Some light must be coming into the room above from the outside. It was toward this light that she climbed cautiously, one uneven stair at a time.

*   *   *

Back at the dinner party, Bonet had just remarked on Janine's absence. Ahmed's smooth explanation of her sudden indisposition seemed to satisfy him for the moment. He was also very busy greeting some of his late arriving guests from the film company. Dinner was delayed for a few minutes while these film folk were given their obligatory aperitif. While they were drinking, Bonet kept a watchful eye on Brian and Ahmed.

Melanie had deserted their party early on the arm of one of the young actors. She had last been seen following him around the house like a new attachment. Once aperitifs were again offered, dinner was finally served on small round tables arranged in the dining room and in the center courtyard. Hordes of white clad waiters then brought in steaming plates of food, *Brique* and *Tanjine* to start, and delicate brochettes of lamb and vegetables. Wine was served in copious quantities.

Ahmed sat with Brian at a table near the corner of the room, and they were joined by some of the film folk, obviously enthralled by Bonet's hospitality. Brian glanced at Ahmed nervously. Janine had been gone for some time now. If she was still in the house, every minute she stayed made her more vulnerable.

*   *   *

Janine had almost reached the top of the stairs. The long *safsari* made each step treacherous. The backless Arab sandals caught on every step, causing her to hug the wall and proceed slowly for fear of falling. There was a dank odor in the stairwell that spoke of centuries of dust and accumulated grime. Finally she reached the room at the top. It was large and rectangular. A single window looked seaward. It was from this window that the soft gray light came.

As she made her way toward it, she realized that it was the light of the rising moon. The floor was cluttered with objects, some of them large and draped with cloths. When she looked under those nearest the window, she realized that these too were Greek and Roman antiquities, probably taken from some of the archaeological sites in Tunisia. It looked like a king's ransom of stolen statues and other artifacts. So this was Bonet's secret passion and one of the reasons that he came to D'Jerba so often. He was either a dealer or a receiver of stolen art objects. This was a side of his business that none of them had even suspected.

A rapid search of the rest of the room didn't immediately reveal the briefcase holding the triggering device. Now that she had uncovered Bonet's secret passion, she doubted if he would have secreted the briefcase here among his art treasures. It might have been too dangerous. And he would not have wanted anyone who worked for him to know of this secret cache. The penalties for stealing antiquities were severe, and if Bonet were a known dealer, he would no longer be welcome in the country. This would be quite a set-back to his other activities.

She covered the statues again with care. After one more look around for the missing briefcase, she moved cautiously down the stairs. Going down was even more treacherous. Now there was no light at all to guide her. She took off the sandals and tucked them under her arm. Barefoot, she made more rapid progress until she again reached the door. She cautiously pushed against it and was relieved to feel that it was still unlatched. She could again see the glowing statue of the Greek boy in the middle of the room.

Suddenly, something was pushing against the door from the other side, and it was slowly closing. She pushed against it with all her force, but the other person was much stronger. She heard a loud click as the door slammed shut and another sound as it was firmly locked behind her. She was trapped in Bonet's tower.

* * *

As the dinner party continued, Brian could see that, despite his stoic exterior, Ahmed was getting more and more concerned about Janine. If she had found anything, she had not returned to the party as promised. Bonet had not left his guests unattended except to nod at one of the servants and to dispatch him on an errand. He was the picture of a relaxed host, reveling in the company of the film actors. Brian had never seen a man who seemed so in charge of the situation. It was hard to believe that he might be mixed up in something that the CIA would be interested in. He seemed the picture of the perfect man of the world and an avid art collector.

By the time desert was served, and rose water was being sprinkled on the guests hands in traditional fashion, Brian was really worried, and he could see that Ahmed shared his discomfort. The tall Arab rose gracefully from his place at the low table, and begging to be excused because of military duties, took Brian with him and made his exit while the musicians were ushered in and coffee was being served.

"Because he is a Frenchman, he will not even know that we are insulting him," Ahmed said, through clenched teeth, as they walked rapidly through the jasmine laden air to the front garden. He glanced toward the tower at the back of the house. There was no sign of life from it, and the moon was now high enough so that the whole garden was brightly illuminated.

"Let's hope she got away before the moon came up," Brian said with a worried frown.

Ahmed looked at him in disgust. "Bonet's men will not need moonlight to shoot her if they find her. Let's hope that she used her head and went directly back to the hotel."

"Then she is in real danger?" Brian asked anxiously.

"Let us say that she is too brave for a woman, and that her sex will not protect her tonight." Ahmed eased his aching shoulder. "Let us take one look at that tower before we leave. In case there is another way in from the garden. We may need this information later."

The two men walked quietly to the back of the garden, through fragrant bushes and birds of paradise, looking strangely alive in the moonlight. A guardian in a white *gelaba* was making tea over a small brazier in the rear of the garden. He looked up curiously as they passed but made no effort to stop them. Their reconnoiter was in vain. There was no entrance to the tower from the outside, and only one window at the very top. As they watched, the window opened slowly and a long white *safsari* was lowered out of it, like a flag.

Ahmed drew in his breath sharply. "She's up there. We need to get her out right away, and alive if we can."

"But how?" Brian asked. "That tower looks like it is several stories high, and I don't see anything around here that looks like a ladder that would reach that far."

"Then we'll get one and come back," Ahmed said through clenched teeth. "Better still, you stay here and keep an eye on that tower in case she tries to jump or something equally stupid. Bonet won't deal with her until his guests leave and that gives us at least another hour." He gave Brian his pistol. "If anyone asks you what you are doing here tell them that you were told to escort Miss Weston back to the hotel. As a matter of fact that might not be such a bad idea if you can pry her away from that actor." He spat out the word as though it were an irritating olive pit.

Brian settled down with his back against a tree and his eyes on the tower. He felt a surge of adrenaline at being given a weapon, and at last having a part to play in this drama. He knew that something big was going on. Janine was too cool a customer to be risking her neck if it weren't important. He hunched down in the shadows, keeping a close watch on the old guardian. The perfume of flowers was almost overwhelming. Perhaps, he mused, this was the scent that had overcome Ulysses and kept him from going home.

The *safsari* was being slowly withdrawn from the window. He thought that he caught a glimpse of Janine's bright head just before the *safsari* vanished. He longed to signal her that he was on guard below, and that he would give his life to keep anything from happening to her. He fingered the pistol that Ahmed had given him, and settled back against the tree again to watch, every nerve taut, the blood of his Virginia ancestors pounding in his veins. This was a night for action and at last he was included in it.

After a few minutes he realized that Janine already had the matter well in hand. The *safsari* appeared again at the window. But this time there were several more pieces tied to it. It came a long way from hitting the ground, but Janine had shortened her jump by about fifteen feet if that was what she was intending to do. Brian moved cautiously toward the tower, holding his breath and clutching the pistol tight against his side. He could see Janine's head again peering out from the tower window and measuring the jump.

Again the *Safsari* was hauled in from the top and a few minutes went by while she added more length to it. The old guardian looked up from his tea as though sensing that something was amiss. Brian froze in his tracks and melted into the bushes. He wouldn't help Janine by calling attention to what she was trying to do. He only hoped that she didn't break her neck while trying to escape from the tower. There was nothing he could do but wait.

Chapter Seventeen

Ahmed raced back toward the hotel like a man possessed. It angered him that Bonet had outwitted him at every turn. The man was a dangerous enemy, to himself and to the Arab world. The kind of parasite that made money out of other people's troubles. He longed to barge into Bonet's home and confront him in front of his guests. But until he had the triggering device in hand he had no proof. He only hoped that Janine had discovered it in the tower.

He needed some rope and a ladder. But where to find them at this time of night he wasn't certain. He stopped at the first date farm he passed, and asked the farmer to sell him some rope. The man looked astonished, and Ahmed realized that in his dress uniform with his arm in a sling, he must look a strange sight to a local date grower. The man had rope, but no ladder. He did have a son however who could climb the tallest date tree and he offered to lend his services to Ahmed, for a price.

*   *   *

Janine had almost exhausted the dust covers in the room. Most of them were old and some were half rotten, but she had managed to find enough to fashion a rude kind of rope. The moonlight that now flooded the room revealed one statue after another of breathtaking beauty. There were also sculpted heads on pedestals, entire mosaic pictures on the floor, and gold framed Arab calligraphy of museum quality hanging on the walls. Removing the last piece of heavy muslin from a statue in the far corner, her foot struck something. It was the briefcase. She stood dumbstruck for a moment. It had been here all the time, and she would have left it. Now she had to manage to get down from the tower, and take it with her. It was their only clear evidence against Bonet. She rigged a sort of sling over her shoulder and placed the briefcase in it, resting it against her back. Then she tied the last of the dust covers together.

The garden looked empty, except for the glow from a small fire and the huddled figure of an old man. He almost looked as though he were sleeping. She checked her pistol again, and then slowly pulled with all her strength against her manufactured rope, testing the strength of each of the knots. One of them slipped loose and she retied it carefully. The home-made rope didn't reach more than three quarters of the way to the ground. But the garden was mostly sand with built up beds of flowers and cactus. She would try land on the sand and escape the cactus.

It was hard to see what was immediately below. She caught her breath. It was now or never. Whoever had locked her in the room would be back soon. And their intentions would be more than just to frighten her this time. She knew that Bonet was playing for very high stakes, and now that she had found his secret treasure cache, she was certainly on his list to be eradicated.

She lowered herself carefully over the window ledge, hugging the *safsari* to her and blessing its hand woven strength. The briefcase cut into her back, bruising her ribs. She took one look below, and then decided that it was safer not to look down. She had passed the end of the *safsari* now, and she felt the second knot slipping through her hands. The night air was cool and a scent of jasmine came up from the garden below. She heard a loud throbbing sound, and realized that it was her own heart beating.

She braced her bare feet against the outer wall and began to rappel slowly down the side. One of her feet scraped against an outcropping and began to bleed, but she continued down. Now she was almost at the end of the rope. She lowered her feet and hung for a moment, swinging freely on the end of the rope, forcing herself to relax and prepare for the drop.

The briefcase was awkward against her back, and would probably injure her if she fell against it. But she had no way to drop it first unless she could hold her own weight with one hand while she released it, hoping that the noise wouldn't alert the old man. She hung suspended for a moment, her arms crying for release. She forced herself to let go with one hand, and as she did so the other slid off the knot at the end of the rope. She fell with the briefcase, landing in a heap in the sand at the bottom of the tower.

She lay there for a moment, with the breath knocked totally out of her. She saw stars against the black sky and her head reeled. Someone was shaking her gently, and pulling her into the shadow of the bushes. She looked into Brian's worried blue eyes, and then lost consciousness. When she came to a few seconds later, Brian was holding her in a sitting position and patting her face anxiously.

"Briefcase", she whispered with what breath she had left. "Got to get the briefcase."

"Got it", Brian answered grimly. "You guard it here while I get rid of your escape route if I can." He tugged on the home-made rope fiercely, and the major part of it came down on top of him. He quickly pulled it into the bushes where Janine was hidden. "We've got to get out of here before the party breaks up," he whispered hurriedly. "That guard must be either deaf of asleep. But if Bonet comes out of the house, I don't think that we want to be found trespassing in his garden."

"Especially with his stolen goods in our possession", Janine whispered. "But how are we going to get out of here. I'm not sure that I can walk."

"Then I'll carry you," Brian said manfully. "I don't think that this is a very healthy place for either one of us to get caught. Lean on me and see if you can move."

Janine moved. Every step was painful and the bottoms of her feet stung as though they had been totally stripped of skin. One of her arms felt as through it was pulled out of its socket. But she could move. She gave Brian the briefcase, and followed him slowly to the front of the garden, gravel stinging her wounded feet.

They could hear sounds from the house, the high pitched strains of Arab music mingled with the sound of laughter and conversation. The guard was asleep, his head sunk into his chest and a cup of tea still held loosely in his right hand.

A number of cars were parked by the front gate, some with chauffeurs waiting beside them. The men were engaged in some kind of game, and hardly looked up as Brian and Janine walked past them. By now Janine was leaning against Brian as though she were slightly drunk. Brian engaged one of the men in conversation, and offered him some dinars to take them back to the hotel, saying that "Madame was *fatigue*." The man smiled knowingly, but refused politely, saying that he had to wait for the film crew as he worked for them.

Just then the young film star strolled out of the shadows, having escaped temporarily from the party and Melanie. He took one look at Janine and realized that something was very wrong. Her dress was torn and streaked with dust and blood. He climbed into the limo with the chauffeur, and ordered the man to take them back to their hotel. Then he grinned at Brian. "Whatever has happened here, I really don't want to know. But you should take better care of your girl friends."

Brian started to answer, but Janine elbowed him in the ribs. Anything it took to get out of firing distance of Bonet and his men was all right with her. The main thing was that Brian was still holding firmly onto the briefcase, and she was alive. The big limo eased its way out of the gate, just as Ahmed came rattling up in the date farmer's wagon. He took one look at Janine and Brian in the limo, quickly turned his clattering vehicle around and followed them down the road back toward their hotel.

The date farmer was astonished at his good fortune. He had made several dinars for not doing much, except lending the officer his truck, and his son, for an hour. He thanked Allah that the people from Tunis were so crazy. He gladly drove Ahmed back to his hotel, without asking for any more money.

Janine found the message from Rick waiting for her under the door when she got to her cabana, after sending Brian firmly off to his room. The young Virginian seemed to feel some sort of responsibility for her now that annoyed her. Despite Ahmed's protests she kept the briefcase with her. Having almost broken her neck to get it, she wasn't about to surrender it to the Tunisians until she had contacted Sam. Ahmed, feeling outmaneuvered for the moment, backed down.

Janine took the case into the bathroom with her, and drew a tub of scalding hot water. Her white kaftan was shredded and streaked with dirt and blood, and her feet felt as though she had been walking on razor blades. She lowered herself into the tub cautiously, and winced as her body hit the water.

It was clear that Bonet was into smuggling in a big way. He was probably responsible for the diversion of Weston chemicals through Tunisia into other countries. The big question was how much did Duke Weston know about all of this, and how deeply was he implicated. If he was one of the dealers in this poker game, that could put a hold on diplomatic relations between Tunisia and the United States for a long time. Weston was well connected, however, and it would be hard to pin anything on him. Perhaps that was why Sam was playing this one so close to his chest.

And what to do about this triggering device? She couldn't let Ahmed confiscate it. Perhaps the best answer was just to take it out and drop it into the gulf of Gabez. She turned the hot water on again, and sank down to chin level, thinking. Then she picked up her cell phone off the toilet and called Rick at his hotel.

The telephone rang several times before Rick awoke. He had been dreaming that they were still in the desert and that he could hear Robbie's cries for help. He turned on the light and answered the telephone, relieved to see the boy still sleeping peacefully. After hearing a carefully edited version of Janine's story, he agreed to meet her downstairs in an hour at his hotel.

"I'd like to bring the merchandise with me, if you don't mind," she said sweetly. "I need a little help figuring out what to do with the evidence."

"Why don't you also bring your nightie and plan to stay here tonight," Rick said amiably. "Your friends may come looking for you when they find that something is missing. Sounds like you've had enough fun for one evening."

"Good idea," Janine agreed. "I'll put on my house slippers and come right over."

She called a taxi and waited in her room until she could see its lights reflected through the sheer drapes. Her feet were still throbbing, but she was able to wear her beach thongs, jeans and a sweater. She tucked the brief case under her arm, her purse under the other, and slid out of her room and into the taxi before Ahmed's door could open. She saw him standing in the doorway peering into the night as the taxi pulled away.

Rick met her at the door of his room, and after nodding for quiet in Robbie's direction, cleared his things off the one arm chair in the room and offered it to her. She slumped into it gratefully. Her arm was throbbing from the effort of carrying the briefcase, and her feet hurt. She glanced at the sleeping Robbie. "So you found him after all?"

"Yes, but not quite all in one piece," he answered honestly. "He doesn't quite remember who he is or why he's here. But he's not as paranoid as when I picked him up."

"Drugs?" Janine asked.

"And other things," Rick answered. "But that's a long story, and the real problem now is how to get the two of you out of here and back to the relative safety of Tunis before Bonet's men appear."

"Relative is probably right as long as I'm carrying this briefcase around," Janine answered. "I want you to help me drop it into the Mediterranean."

Rick looked slightly amused. "Is that the Agency's new way of getting rid of things they don't know what to do with?" He grinned at her affably. "My suggestion is that we take it back to Tunis, and send it to Langley in the diplomatic pouch. No one will be any the wiser that it has left the country, and the good news is that none of the Arab states, including the friendly ones, will get their hands on it." He smiled down at her. "You will be a heroine with the Agency for having gotten it back. It might even mean a promotion."

Janine considered his proposition for a few minutes. If they could get back to Tunis with the triggering device intact, and themselves as well, Rick's idea just might work. The diplomatic pouch was sacrosanct—no one but high level Embassy personnel had access to it and none of the Tunisians. The triggering device could be out of the country, and on its way back to a secure depot, before Bonet and his men had time to trace it. "But what about Bonet, do we let him just slip through our fingers?" she pondered.

"Let the Tunisians take care of him. When Ahmed makes his report Bonet's sure to be named '*persona non grata*', and shipped out of the country with his visa pulled for a long long time." He patted her hand. "Don't worry. You know they have an excellent intelligence service. They've probably just been waiting for Bonet to slip up enough so that they could throw him and his men out of the country. Having once been a French colony themselves, they have no great love for the '*pied noir*'."

Janine glanced over at him in the half-light. His face seemed thinner than she remembered and there were circles of exhaustion under his eyes. He glanced often at the sleeping figure of the boy in the corner. It was a look filled with a father's concern, and something more that she couldn't read. "What about Robbie's grandfather, Duke Weston? How is he involved in this?" she asked.

Rick considered the question for a minute. Then he leaned over closer to her. "I guess that the buck stops on his desk, whether he knew about what Bonet was doing or not. It won't go well with his reputation, or his trade relations with the Tunisians. But frankly Scarlet, I don't give a damn. Whatever fall-out there is over this is long overdue." He dropped his hand lightly on her shoulder, caressing her neck gently.

"And Robbie and Melanie?" Janine asked, sinking back into the chair, her eyes half closing in fatigue as he rubbed her shoulder.

"Only time will tell about Robbie. Melanie still has legal custody of him until he's eighteen, and the Embassy doctor seems to have a line on his problem," he answered, putting one arm around her. "Maybe it's time she learned how to pay some real attention to him for a change. And I plan not to be an absentee father anymore. Whatever treatment he needs we'll get it for him."

"In other words a commitment to him, whatever happens."

"Isn't that what fathers are for?" Rick asked, making room for himself beside her in the chair and taking her firmly into his lap.

* * *

Ambassador Olgelvie stood on the tarmac in the late afternoon sun, bidding farewell to his Commercial Attaché, who was on her way back to Washington to receive a commendation and, probably, a promotion.

He was annoyed at having to miss his afternoon tennis game, as well as having to extend hospitality to Duke Weston's daughter and grandson for a few more days. He was delighted that the boy had been found, and that the Embassy doctor had been able to recommend a series of treatments that seemed to be working.

The boy looked less like a wraith and more like a normal teenager everyday. But his father was a strange chap. Seemed to be in a big hurry to get back to Washington himself, and was accompanying the Commercial Attaché on her flight today. He insisted in carrying his own luggage, which consisted of a large black metal briefcase. Probably some commercial samples. After all the man did represent a fertilizer company. Strange thing for an ex-CIA agent to be doing. But then as he always told Mrs. Olgelvie, there was just no accounting for tastes.

Rick was the last to board the big airplane. His company, relieved to have him back, had reserved a first class ticket for him back to Washington, and then on to company headquarters. Janine was sitting in the last row of first class, attractively attired in a raw silk suit and white tennis shoes. After putting his briefcase in the overhead rack, he sat down beside her and took her hand in his. She didn't pull it away, but looked up questioningly in the direction of the luggage rack.

"Isn't that tempting fate? I thought that the ambassador was going to put it in the Diplomatic pouch."

"He did," Rick answered.

"Then what's in the briefcase?"

"Would you believe…. fertilizer samples."

"Then you're not worried that I saw what looked like two of Bonet's men getting on in tourist class?"

"Not a bit. When we get to Washington, I intend to leave it on the plane as a present for them. And when they take if off, some of the good guys will be waiting for them. Now what would you like with your champagne Miss Sims? We've got ten hours before we get to Washington. Shall we start by getting our stories straight before we talk to Sam?"

About the Author

Anne Kimbell has lived in Tunisia and in the Republic of Chad, Africa. She has written for *The Foreign Service Journal* and for *The Christian Science Monitor* as well as a popular book " How To Communicate With Difficult People, " She lives in Laguna Beach California in the winter and in Westcliffe Colorado in the summer where she is the Artistic Director of The Crystal Mountain Center for the Performing Arts. www.crystlmtn.org